Little Reminders of Who I Will Become

Also by Jeff S. Bray

The Five Barred Gate
The Transference

Little Reminders of Who I Am
Little Reminders of Who I Was
Little Reminders of Who I Will Become

Little Reminders
of Who I Will Become

Jeff S. Bray

WordCrafts Press

Little Reminders of Who I Will Become
Copyright © 2023
Jeff S. Bray

ISBN: 978-1-962218-17-7

Cover art by Carolyn Bray at Colorful Creations by Carolyn
Cover design by David Warren

Published by WordCrafts Press
Cody, Wyoming 82414
www.wordcrafts.net

Little Reminders
of Who I Will Become

Jeff S. Bray

WordCrafts Press

To the memory of my sister, Jennifer Bray.
Her love of the ocean will forever live in the sands of time.
Love you, li'l sis.

Prologue

"So, where do we go from here?" Carter asked Gabriel.

"That's up to you. Are you ready for another assignment so soon?"

"I need to keep busy. One can only read for so long."

"Carter Jennings, are you saying you're getting tired of books?"

"Not at all. I'm just saying I'd rather live them."

"Well, how is this for living?" Gabriel produced another shoebox, just the kind Carter liked to use, and handed it to him. "Have you ever read Charles Dickens?"

"You mean?" Carter said, peeking inside the shoebox and quickly shutting it. "Are you serious?"

"I am an angel of the Lord. I'm always serious." Gabriel stood, removing his cap and coat. His angelic appearance was restored. He looked back down at Carter with his crystal blue eyes.

"One day, you will have to teach me how you do that," Carter said.

Gabriel laughed. Even his laughter sounded heavenly. "So, what do you say, Carter? You up to *this* adventure?"

Carter looked again into the shoebox and grinned, "I wouldn't miss this for the world."

Two weeks later

"So, refresh an old angel's memory, Gabriel. How will this work?" Carter said, sitting across from him in a library corner.

Gabriel was wearing one of his disguises—this time a Carolina Panther's hoodie and sweatpants. It was his idea to meet in this fashion. Why was beyond him? Perhaps he had gotten a taste of what he had experienced talking to Aaron and enjoyed the thrill of a deep cover assignment.

"It's simple. You have a little less than a week to work with Stephanie Marshall. And you'll need all five days because there is a schedule. First, you spend two days here to set everything up. Then you'll have one day in the past, and one day back here in the present, then you'll have one in the future. Finally, Stephanie will experience one day back here in the present, where you will tie everything together for her."

"Wow," Carter said, eyebrows raised. "You call that simple?"

"Okay, I know, it's a lot in a little time. It's by far the most arduous task you've undertaken. He's never asked you to show someone their life in this fashion, let alone in a week's time."

"Where is she spiritually?" Carter asked.

"You'll see. The short version is that Stephanie grew up in church but fell away when her parents died in a car accident when she was twelve. Her husband brought her back to the Lord while they were dating, but it was half-hearted." Gabriel handed him a newspaper that had tomorrow's date. "Stephanie Marshall is a writer and graphic designer for a growing firm and is away from home for long hours."

"Ah," Carter said. He thumbed through the paper, and Gabriel directed him to Stephanie's article. Carter nodded, skimming it. "Is there temptation of an affair at her work?"

"You're good at this," Gabriel nodded. "Stephanie hasn't crossed that line—yet," Gabriel said.

"Now I understand more about the items in the box. These will be interesting to place since I will most likely be with her the entire time."

"Well, that's the beauty of these items," Gabriel said. "They are different than your normal reminders. These are transcendent for you. You place them here, and they will be there, wherever and *whenever* you place them. So, she, and only she, can find them. He will see to that." Gabriel nodded to the sky.

Carter followed his gaze and grinned. "Even in the past?'

"You doubt Him?"

"Not in the least. This should be exciting. How will the shifting work for her?"

"This is where it will get interesting. You'll find this part will vary. God will show you along the way. So be prepared."

"But no time machines, buttons to push, or fancy gadgets?" Carter asked.

"No, nothing like that, Carter," Gabriel laughed.

"Good. You know me. My wristwatch is as high-tech as I get," Carter said, looking at his wrist.

"But you don't wear a wristwatch," Gabriel said.

"Exactly," Carter said, pointing at his friend.

Gabriel laughed. "Okay, now. This is where you come in. You have a bit more latitude than usual. Your identity has normally been top secret. Here you have full authority to reveal who you are, just not *why* you're there. Not that that has prevented you from tipping your hat before, but here it is fully sanctioned. Remember, with Stephanie, you have two days to approach her and let her know what's coming."

"She won't believe me."

"Of course not," Gabriel said with a chuckle. "When do they ever?"

Carter laughed and leaned back in his chair. "In the new time period, will I have to locate her, or will she find me?"

"No. You'll be close by. If you have done your job well, she will come to you."

"Ahh. Okay." Carter leaned over and looked his companion in the eye, "Now, Gabe, you're not going to interfere with *this* assignment, are you? I know you have gotten a taste of the comfort of sweatshirts and ball caps, but as you know, Heaven is far more comfortable. Maybe God can give you an outfit that matches your robe?"

Gabriel stood and looked around. Once he was convinced their corner was private enough, he closed his eyes, and with a flash, his heavenly appearance was restored, blue eyes glowing at Carter.

"I *love* how you do that," Carter said, slapping his hands and rubbing them together.

Gabriel placed his hand on Carter's shoulder. "Remember, this life was your choice."

"And a wise choice it was," Carter said. "People need the Lord. And God's Little Reminders are bringing so many back to Him. I will continue doing this as long as He needs me to. I'm looking forward to helping Stephanie return to the Lord. Now go back into His presence and say hello for me. Tell Him, *Carter's on the job, and I am pleased to do His will.*"

Chapter
One

"How do these look, Stephanie?" Vanessa asked.

Stephanie sighed. She wasn't happy. The design was still off. This was the third draft she had requested from her free-lancer, and she was growing impatient. Stephanie pointed to the top of the page, "What if we went blue instead of green on the header? And on the date graphic, increase the font to sixteen points instead of fourteen for the year? 2025, just looks off for some reason."

"Will do," Vanessa said as she released an invisible sigh and left the room. Stephanie knew it was because it may have been one of the variations they had reviewed earlier. Schemes often blend, and you never realize the other looked better until you see one that looks worse. Well, now they knew.

"Thank you, Vanessa," Stephanie called out as she scampered down the hall.

Stephanie Marshall was a semi-executive officer of Marshall Copywriting Services, LLC, a small firm, if you could call it that. She was more of a Freelancer that had expanded beyond a home office. Just over a year ago, she had outgrown her ten-by-ten room and leased office space in their small South Carolina town. Jason, her husband, was the most excited about her business venture. His construction firm had been one of her first success stories. He excelled from the articles and advertising that she had contracted. Now the fruits of her labor had grown into her own small business. Vanessa was her first hire and had been with her since the business' conception.

Today, Stephanie had ten major contract clients and at least a dozen assignment-based clients that called on her as needed. Writing was her primary skill, and Vanessa was her graphics guru. She had three other in-house writers, in addition to Vanessa, that worked for her. All had different skills, and with that, she was able to take any client on any topic. Working in-house was one of the prerequisites she wanted for her writers. Remote workers were fine, but an office atmosphere was more conducive to the type of team she wanted. And her staff understood the responsibility and performed well.

After Vanessa, her team consisted of three writers with different expertise levels. Ethan was all about sports. He could write his way out of a paper bag about any topic. From football to *futbol*, that's soccer to American-speaking folk. He was also a minor in finance. He knew the lingo and how to convert words into sales, and that was what the client paid the big bucks for them to deliver. Some of their biggest clients were Ethan's.

Lauren had the fun clients. She got to review recipes and even tour restaurants in the local area for the best deals and write about them. Touring was a big part of it, even to the local cities within driving distance. Traveling was fun, and

Lauren was good at finding those hideaway places no one knew about. Many of her pieces were picked up by national publications.

And then there was Kenneth. What could she say about Kenneth? He was a jack-of-all-trades, master of none. There was not a column he couldn't write, not an article he could not piece together, not a human-interest story he couldn't grab a reader from word one. He was so good that he was up for a local award for columnist of the year. She couldn't help but feel proud; she had discovered the talent. She had discovered him in more ways than one.

It was during lunch one afternoon and then an early dinner one evening that she realized how much she was learning about her colleague.

Marshall Copywriting Services, LLC, was lucrative enough to pay its employees well. With her colleagues' awards, Stephanie knew she would continue to have to pay top dollar to keep them around. Although with Kenneth, regardless of pay, he may not be around much longer. His days of mediocre article writing were always a stepping stone for him. He had mentioned it over dinner last week. She enjoyed listening to his aspirations. It was a change of pace from hearing about drywall and building inspections at home—someone who understood the trade and had their eye on something bigger and better.

It wasn't that Stephanie wasn't happy at home. She loved Jason. Their nearly ten years of marriage had been blissful. Two kids and a beautiful home that he practically built himself. It had all the amenities she desired and even planned herself. They had no marital issues. Jason treated her well, they never argued, things were just—stale. It was routine. They both came home, talked about their day as they ate dinner, watched television, dealt with the kids, and then went to bed. It was what she wanted, or so she thought. It came to the point where she stayed at the office a bit longer, where a simple offer to grab a drink became attractive.

Kenneth was almost ten years her junior. And for a woman in her mid-thirties, eyeing a boy just passing the legal limit seemed daring. You could almost say it flattered her that a younger man found her attractive. She was trying to remember the last time Jason had complimented her when she got her hair done or noticed a blouse she was excited about purchasing. While Kenneth wasn't quick to notice either, when the girls complimented her, he would be quick to agree with their assessment. Either way, it was flattering.

Last night they had their latest after work drink. She wouldn't call it *cheating* on Jason. They never crossed any lines. It wasn't like they were having sex; they hadn't even shared a kiss. The most that had happened was he took her hand when they walked into the restaurant. She had to admit though, it sent her heart fluttering when he made the gesture. Stephanie wondered if anyone else at the office knew of their after-work meetings. They did their best to keep it secret. But she would often catch herself holding a glance at Kenneth too long and have to break it. If one of the team noticed, she didn't know.

Stephanie felt it was innocent enough. All they did was talk about work at their dinners. They never discussed taking the next step in their relationship... if that was what it was. No. All business. For that, right now, she was grateful. She knew it eventually had to end, or it would proceed to the next step. And as a Christian, adultery was a big no-no. Right now, she was still in the safe zone. She had not crossed that *fine line.*

Ethan entered her office, tossing a thumb drive to her. "Heads up, boss."

Even in her daze, Stephanie caught it, as she always did, and laughed. "Can't get one past me, E."

"One day, Step-on-me."

"Oh, for heaven's sake. What are you, four?"

Ethan laughed. He was actually twenty-six. Their office antics were one reason she hired young, well, younger. Older staff was more concerned about who they could step on and move up the ladder. She once voiced that opinion to her team. Thus, the nickname. But she took the ribbing in stride. True, she was their boss, and there was some level of insubordination to the office antics, but they knew where the line was, and they kept within it.

"I'll let you know if it needs any edits," she called to him.

"Won't need it, Steph."

She knew it wouldn't. Ethan was a perfectionist and top of his game, just like the others. She could hit send without looking at it, but she wouldn't be doing her job if she did. And it was what the clients paid her to do.

After a half hour of combing, the page had two errors, but they were simple and could go either way. More of her preference than Ethan's mistake. She made the corrections and submitted it to their client.

She shut down her computer and waited. She knew Kenneth was about to come by her office any moment. She had told Jason she had a meeting with a client to possibly sign them on. It would mean a lucrative deal. Hit and miss was always the game for freelancing. This one would be a miss.

But maybe not for her. She watched her screen as the spinning wheel showed her the shutdown process was doing what it should be, and there was a knock at her door.

"Hey," the brown-eyed man with slightly unkempt hair stared at her. "You about ready?"

Stephanie turned off the screen and the desk light. "Yeah," she said but remained seated.

Kenneth stepped into the office, "You, okay?" His eyebrows raised.

Stephanie sighed. That prickling of a conscience gnawed at her again. But it was no longer as strong as it had been. She had overcome the stabbing it had given her in the past. And the photos that had been on the desk haunting her—those were now on the shelf behind her. They were no longer there to preach at her.

Kenneth smiled, extending his hand. She relaxed, accepted his hand, and stood as he brought her in for an embrace. Stephanie wondered what the taste of his kiss would be like.

"Ahem," a voice cleared behind them. It was Vanessa. "Sorry, boss, I need you to sign these payroll forms. They need to go out today so that we can be paid on Friday. You said to remind you before you headed out. I saw your light turn off, and I thought you were leaving. I apologize." She placed the form on the end table near the door and quickly disappeared.

"Dang it," Stephanie said.

"Is that going to be a problem?" Kenneth said, stepping back to a safe distance.

"Not at all. She's a vault. But *I* will know."

"I ask again, is this going to be a problem, Steph?"

Stephanie sat at an office chair, placing her hands behind her neck.

"Maybe we should forget about tonight, Kenneth," she said, looking up at him.

"You sure? You said she was a vault. If she doesn't say anything, I don't see why we should let it spoil our evening."

"I know. I know. I just don't feel up to it now. I'm sorry."

"Raincheck?" Kenneth asked.

"Yeah," Stephanie said.

"Okay. See you next week," Kenneth said, then left her office.

Stephanie realized how low she had been. Now she had been caught. Not that it mattered with Vanessa. It was true, Vanessa wouldn't say anything to anyone. She was not one for office gossip. Stephanie doubted she would even mention it to her husband—if she had one.

It made Stephanie think. She knew little about Vanessa other than her work ethic. For that matter, she didn't know anything about anyone in her office. But wasn't that how it should be? Work was work, and personal life was just that. And now she had just brought that to the forefront and exposed the one thing she couldn't admit to herself; sex or no sex, call a spade a spade, she was having an affair.

Chapter
Two

Wednesday, November 19, 2025

"Guess it didn't go well," Jason said, washing his hands.

Stephanie headed straight to the closet to change into pajamas. She needed to get out of her work clothes and the scent Kenneth left on her. She didn't want to take the chance of Jason hugging her and asking questions. She could smell him in the car on the way home. It held her in a daze between ecstasy and shame. Stephanie knew she wasn't in a good place, but she couldn't help herself. She wanted to quit, but when she looked into Kenneth's eyes, she saw herself ten years younger and running away from the bonds of monotony.

"No, it didn't even get started. They called and said they chose to go with another company and didn't want to waste our time," Stephanie said, biting her lip. She hated to lie, but what could she do?

"Sorry to hear, babe," Jason met her at the closet door. "You'll get 'em next time." He hugged her, kissing her on the cheek.

She could've sworn she heard a sniff.

Jason left her to finish dressing. "Dinner's in the microwave. I made you a plate before I put everything away. Chicken parmesan."

"Thank you," she said, putting her pants and blouse at the bottom of the hamper. She shook her head. At least if she had been with a client, she could explain the smell from the valet at the restaurant.

After washing her makeup off—and any lingering scent— she went downstairs. Jason was watching the end of a game. She couldn't tell who the Hornets were playing; she wasn't a sports fan. That was another thing that attracted her to Kenneth. Even though he was an avid writer, sports wasn't his thing. He couldn't tell you the difference between DiMaggio and DiGiorno. Now that it was November, Jason would be lost to the middle of the football season. Although tonight it was basketball, she would be lucky if her husband noticed her sitting next to him.

Stephanie headed to the kitchen to heat leftovers. One thing that Jason was good for was he was one heck of a cook. Even though the game was on, he would never just throw a pizza in the oven or nuke something for Evelyn and Joshua. Stephanie looked up at the ceiling. Both kids were probably lost in video games or television by now. She had been so wrapped up in erasing evidence she had forgotten to knock on their doors. She put the plate her husband had prepared into the microwave, set the timer, and headed back upstairs.

Joshua was seven and definitely a big brother to his little sister, Evelyn, who was five. It was her first year in kinder-garten, and Josh had prepared, getting ready to protect her at school. Perhaps overdoing it at times. He recently had a little bit of trouble over defending a friend against a bully. They explain fighting isn't always the best solution. They hoped he understood but would not get bent out of shape if he were to get caught again standing up for someone smaller, like his little sister.

Getting Evelyn to go to school was not as difficult as they had anticipated. They had Joshua to thank for most of the success. He talked about school as if it was the most fun place on earth. She went the first day with stars in her eyes. They were waiting for the stars to turn to tears when she realized school wasn't as great as her big brother made it out to be, but that day hadn't come. It had been a little over two months, and they were both still waiting for that shoe to drop. They would handle it when it did.

As she approached Joshua's room, she could hear the two talking about what homework was. Apparently, Joshua had it, and Evelyn couldn't understand why the teacher expected you to take school home with you.

Stephanie had to laugh. Their little girl was just beginning to understand life and the whole education process. She knocked on the door.

"Mommy!" Evelyn said, jumping out of bed and into Stephanie's arms. "You will never guess what."

"What is that sweetie?"

"I got to draw a giraffe today."

"Really?" Stephanie said. "Were you able to bring it home so I could see it?"

"No. The teacher put them on the wall at the school. She said you will see them later."

"I look forward to it," Stephanie said, setting Evelyn down. "What about you, buddy? What does your agenda look like?"

"What's an agenda?" Evelyn said.

"It's a list of what you need to do, sis," Joshua said.

"Very good, Joshua," Stephanie said. "One of your vocabulary words?"

"Like last year, Mom," Joshua said. "Old word."

"Gotcha. My bad," Stephanie said, laughing. "What are we studying tonight?"

"Ugh. Math." Joshua rolled his eyes.

"Your dad would be better at that," Stephanie said. "I write. He does math."

"He's busy," Josh said, his face downcast, looking toward the door.

Stephanie was a bit upset with Joshua's statement. She wondered if he had been downstairs and how many times a preoccupied father had shooed him off. She shook her head, making a note to address the issue with Jason. A son's homework should take priority over the latest scores. Her husband could be near perfect in one area, like dinner, but lacking in others—kids and homework.

"Let's take a look," Stephanie said, reaching out her hand.

Half an hour later, Josh's homework was completed, and both kids were ready for bed. So was she. It had been a long and exhausting day. Stephanie wanted to take care of one more chore before the day was through. She wanted to get the tainted hamper down to the laundry room. Better safe than sorry. She found a few more items lying around to make a full load and not draw suspicion of doing a partial load.

"Any work pants, love?" Stephanie asked.

"Oh, yeah. I have a pair next to the washer," he said, pointing but not looking at her. Stephanie rolled her eyes, knowing she was in the clear. She could've waved the blouse in the air, and he wouldn't have noticed. What was she worried about?

Stephanie started the load and reheated the plate that had cooled with her activities upstairs. She took her plate and sat on the couch across from him while he finished the game. During commercials, she asked him about his current project.

"We're waiting on the AC inspector to check their guy's work. Once that's done, we can begin sheet rock. The electric work is complete. Plumbing is complete. The water is on. The owner is antsy because he just wants to move in. We are on schedule, but you know new homeowners. They want it done yesterday."

It was true. In every project, she remembered Jason always complaining about the property owner giving him grief about moving in. She even recalled giving him grief about moving into their own home when they were building the place they were living in now. Stephanie looked up and around. Jason built it nearly by himself. There was no home like it in town. The floor-plan was custom, and everything was just like she had dreamed. Jason was effective at what he did. He and his partner, Blake, knew the industry and built half of the community they lived in.

Marshall Contracting was well known in Evansville, North Carolina. It's substantial growth was partly due to Stephanie. She had written articles and promotional material for his company. It was how they met. Jason took her to dinner as part of his thank you for her services. He eventually confessed that he had other intentions, she expressed a mutual attraction, and the rest was history. Dinner, courting, marriage, kids— now this. Stephanie looked around again with a quiet sigh. She remembered the days when she mattered over the scores.

Jason did at one time have a romantic side. When they dated, he would do all the little things that captured her attention. On their first date their ice breaker was a menu. Silly, yes, but he later showed her that menu. He had kept it as a keepsake. She was flattered by the gesture. He kept it framed on his office wall, until a break-in destroyed it. That loss broke his heart. She had been meaning to replace it, but time and life always got in the way. Who knew if it still had meaning to him anyhow.

Another commercial aired, and he grunted. She supposed the game was not going his team's way. "Sorry your meeting didn't go your way tonight," he said.

A pang of guilt hit her again as she finished her last bite. "It happens. We'll get the next one—part of the business. But I don't want to talk about it. I just want to rest tonight." She set her plate on the coffee table. "Thank you for making supper."

"No problem. We wrapped up early waiting for the inspector to come out. He never showed, so we called it a day. No one complained."

Stephanie snickered. "Yeah, I bet. At least it's cooling down out there."

"Yeah. November can be a crazy month to be out there. The weather won't make up its mind. Summer and Fall still want to fight, even though they know Winter is around the corner. At least *you* get AC."

"True. I don't envy you." Stephanie admired her husband's work ethic, but it was sometimes a bit much. He pulled longer hours than she would prefer. But she couldn't complain too much—she was guilty of the same thing, staying later to meet a deadline, or…

She sighed.

"So, what inning are we in?" she asked, trying to get her mind back on track.

"Steph, this is basketball."

"Oh, right. Quarter. What quarter are we in?"

"About five minutes left in the fourth. It's almost over."

"From the exasperation in your sigh, I can tell your team isn't doing well."

"No, it's pretty much over. There could be a miracle, but I don't see that happening."

"Sorry. Well, better luck tomorrow then."

"Travel day tomorrow. They'll play on Friday."

"Great. Maybe your contractor will come, and you can finish your job and be ready to go on Friday, job complete."

"Here's hoping." Jason lifted his soda, imagined a toast, and sipped his can.

"Well, love, I'm gonna head to bed. It's been a long day, and we have four deadlines tomorrow. If I'm going to have a brain in the morning, I need my sleep." She kissed him on the forehead and ran her hands through his rumpled hair.

"Okay, babe. I'll be up in a bit. Just going to finish this game, then I'll be up," he said. This meant finishing the game and then watching an hour of highlights of why his team lost, reels of each moment of missed plays, and commentary on what they needed to do to win the next game.

Stephanie washed her dish and placed it in the rack next to the sink. She took a Tylenol for her headache and headed upstairs. She passed the kids' doors, both resounding with sleep sounds. Once in bed, she set her alarm. It was true, their writers did have multiple deadlines the next day. She was dreading heading in. How was she to face them knowing what Vanessa knew? It was going to be different now. Lying here was different now. Kenneth and where their relationship was heading wouldn't leave her thoughts. She pretended to be asleep when her husband joined her. She couldn't face him with another man on her mind.

Chapter
Three

Thursday, November 20, 2025

"Good morning, Tiffany. Five coffees. I sent the mobile order."

"Yes, your order was received, Mrs. Marshall. We will get right on it," Tiffany said.

That was one of the benefits of being a writer—and locations knowing you're a writer. You will always got the best service. People feared a critical review. If Tiffany treated her rudely or one of the baristas put too much cinnamon in Lauren's latte, all of North Carolina would hear about it, and Tiffany could be an ex-Latte Loco employee by the end of the week. It was how the world worked. But Stephanie still filtered how her writers vented their frustrations. One over-spiced latte was no reason to *vente* to the entire Evansville community.

"Here is your mocha, Mrs. Marshall. If you'll have a seat, we will have your order out in a few minutes," Tiffany said, handing her a tall cup. The others in line gave her sour glances having to wait a few minutes longer. She took her beverage and sat at a table next to a man in a tweed hat and coat reading a newspaper. He was sipping what appeared to be a cup of black coffee.

She shrugged. *Who drinks black coffee in a fancy coffee shop?*

"How is your mocha, Stephanie?"

The unexpected greeting made Stephanie jump.

"I haven't tasted it yet," she said with a bit of hesitation. Why was this stranger addressing her? Did she know him?

The man lowered his paper. He was older. His white hair peeked from under his hat. He smiled wide through his equally white beard, and his grey eyes beamed.

"I apologize," he said. "I didn't mean to startle you. Just making small talk as we wait."

"Alright," Stephanie said, still unsure what to make of the stranger.

"You are Stephanie Marshall, columnist, am I correct?"

Stephanie released a breath. She realized he was reading the *Evansville Examiner*, where she had a weekly column. It being Thursday, her article would be right about the page he was at. He saw her face, heard Tiffany call her name, and put two and two together. "Yes, sir, I am. Thank you for reading."

"You are a fabulous writer," the man said. "I love to read. And you make it worthwhile if I do say so."

"Thank you, sir.

"The name is Carter Jennings," Carter said, extending his hand.

Stephanie accepted it. Then looked down at his cup. "So, black coffee, Mr. Jennings?"

"I find anything else this early too extravagant."

"I see," Stephanie commented. "So why a coffeehouse? You can get simple coffee anywhere and pay half as much."

"I've heard good things about this place, and I'm always up for trying a location at least once. Now I can add Latte Loco to my list."

"So, you are a connoisseur then," she asked.

"You can say that," Carter said, sipping his cup.

"I'm a bit of one myself," Stephanie said. "And how would you rate this place?"

"It's good, but I wouldn't write home about it," Carter said with a wink.

"And where's home?"

Carter laughed, "I am from here and there."

"And where is there?"

"My last *there* was just south of Houston. A small community, much like this one."

"So, you are a vagabond?"

"Ha. No, far from it. Why, do I look like one?"

Stephanie gave Carter a once over. Then met his eyes. "Well, from the tweed, I would say so, but you are far too clean to be one."

"Thank you. I try to remain hygienic," Carter chuckled.

"Admirable. So, what brings you to Evansville? Work?"

"You can say that."

"And what is work?"

"I like to help people," Carter said plainly.

"Ah. And how is that?"

"With this and that. I find out what they need and help meet that need."

"Mmmhmm," Stephanie said, nodding.

The barista called Stephanie's name.

"Well, Mr. Jennings, it was a pleasure talking to you. I need to get going."

"Pleasure was mine." He smiled. "Oh, and you may want to take this." Carter handed her the paper. You may find something of interest."

"Yes, I know my piece came out today," Stephanie said.

"Well, take it anyway. I insist. It's always good to hold onto something special to us. We never know when something we hold dear will be lost. Then when it's found again, our joy will be inexplicable. Have a pleasant day, Stephanie."

Stephanie didn't understand what Carter meant but accepted the stranger's gift, placing the newspaper under her arm. For some reason, she felt his offer meant something more.

Stephanie handed out coffees and checked on her staff's progress with their deadlines. Clients were anticipating their pieces. It was going to be a busy day. Ethan was in his office with his door shut, which meant, *Do Not Disturb*. He was in final edit mode. That was a good thing. Lauren was singing, which was also a good sign; that meant she was making progress. All was happy on the home front. She looked into Kenneth's office. He wasn't there, so she placed his dark mocha and four sugars on his desk, then she quickly exited to keep from running into him.

To her credit, Vanessa had not mentioned their encounter. She behaved as if it hadn't occurred. It was business as usual, which relieved Stephanie. Perhaps she could get past the moment as well. Maybe she and Kenneth should just cool it for a while to let her get her head on straight. Her guilt was overwhelming at times. Yet, how he made her feel when they were together melted that uneasy feeling away in an instant. It was just a matter of making it past the gate guards of her emotions. She returned to her desk with her hazelnut blend and sat at her desk.

Stephanie removed the lid, and the steam was still there. It occurred to her she hadn't taken a sip while talking with the stranger, which reminded her of his bizarre goodbye as she left the shop. She found the paper he gave her and unfolded it, and as she did something fell to the floor. Stephanie knelt to pick it up. It was a simple laminated sheet— a menu. But it wasn't just any menu; it was *her* menu. And it wasn't a copy of it; it was the one they had lost, the one that Jason had hung on his wall, the one he had cherished for years. She recognized the thumbprint stain in the upper corner that a lazy staff member overlooked before the company had laminated it. They joked about it all night; it was distinguished and made the piece unique. It was *their* menu.

Stephanie nearly dropped her coffee. Then it hit her, "Carter Jennings."

She must've said it out loud because Vanessa heard her and stopped at her door. "Who?"

Great, another name to add to the supposition of her philandering. "Someone I met at the coffee shop this morning gave this to me." She handed Vanessa the menu.

"What is it?"

"It's the menu from the restaurant Jason and I went to on our first date," Stephanie said, her voice still floating in wonder.

"Wow. That is nice. How did he get it?"

"No, you don't understand. That menu used to hang in Jason's office. It was stolen in a robbery two years ago."

"Oh my. You don't think—"

"No. I don't know," Stephanie said, grabbing her wallet. "But I'm going to find out." She headed toward the door.

"Make sure everything is on my desk within the next hour. I'll be right back. I shouldn't be long."

"Gotcha, boss," Vanessa said.

Stephanie darted past a confused Lauren and didn't even notice Kenneth, who had come out of the conference room. She didn't have time to talk to anyone. Her mind was set on finding Carter Jennings.

"No, Mrs. Marshall, I'd never seen him here before today," Tiffany said. "He was here about fifteen minutes before you walked in and left shortly after you did."

"Did he ask about me?"

"No, not at all. Just ordered a black coffee and sat down with his paper."

A paper! "So, he brought the paper with him?"

"Yes."

"Was anything else in his hands?"

Tiffany's face scrunched in thought, then she shook her head. "I'm sorry, Mrs. Marshall. I don't know. I see so many people. I couldn't tell you. I just remember the newspaper. I know because I was looking at what he was wearing. You don't see tweed very often, at least not like his."

"It's okay," Stephanie said. Tiffany wouldn't have seen it anyhow. A simple sheet of paper? *She* almost missed it. If it hadn't been for his elaborate speech, she would've trashed it. "Thanks for your help, Tiffany."

Stephanie turned to leave, but snapped her fingers and turned back to the barista. "Say, if the man in the tweed hat comes back, could you give him my card and ask him to call me? I have a few questions I'd like to ask him?"

"Ohhh, like an interview?"

"Yeah, something like that. I want to ask him about something he gave me."

"Certainly, Mrs. Marshall. You can count on me," Tiffany said, holding onto the card like it was gold.

Stephanie doubted she would see him again. With Carter only being in the place once and his mission to deliver the document complete, he was good as gone. *Was he responsible for the theft? Did he know the person who was? Perhaps. Maybe he's a relative of the person who stole it, and he returned the menu as a peace offering. Now that it was returned, I think it's safe to assume he'll disappear out of fear of prosecution. Yeah, that'll be the last time I see Carter Jennings.*

Chapter
Four

Thursday, November 20, 2025

"And you've never seen this *Carter* guy before?" Jason asked, flipping the menu over, examining it like it was the Declaration of Independence.

"It's the same menu, Jase. I've looked it over a hundred times. Down to the thumbprint."

Jason looked at the print again, "Do you think he knew the person who robbed the office?"

"I don't know. This man was older. He seemed innocent enough. He almost looked homeless."

"Homeless?" Jason asked.

"Yeah. But he was too clean to be homeless. His coat and hat were spotless."

"Coat and hat?"

"Yeah. He was wearing a tweed overcoat and hat. He even *smelled* fresh," Stephanie explained.

"Fresh?"

"Yeah." Stephanie flapped her hands at her sides. "And

I've been around the homeless. You know that smell, even if they've cleaned up. This man was spotless. He was like someone's grandfather."

"So, you think he might know the person who robbed the office?"

"That's my thought. Maybe he found out it was stolen and wanted to return it."

"But why take it out of the frame?" Jason wondered, setting down the menu and picking up his mug.

Stephanie shrugged. "Maybe the thieves took it out of the frame to sell it? Then grandfather saw the menu, understood its sentimental value, and his conscience told him to return it."

"What did he say again?"

Stephanie closed her eyes, relying on her memory, "He said something like 'We never know when something we hold dear will be lost. That when it's found, we will have joy.' No," she corrected herself. "He said, 'when it is found, our joy will be *inexplicable*,' I remember that because it is an uncommon word."

"What do you think it means? It's funny because it explains our situation."

"Well, he knows we lost this because of the theft. Now it's being returned. Makes sense he would say that returning the item." Stephanie explained.

"I suppose," Jason said, smiling, then picking up the menu and staring it again. "I'm just glad to have it back. It sure brings back memories." He paused in thought. "I was so nervous that day."

"Yeah," Stephanie said. She remembered him barely able to get a word out. For some reason, she made him nervous. Not sure if it was first-date jitters or their professional relationship turning personal. It was cute. He dropped his fork a couple of times, all the staple first-date fears. It was the thumb printed menu that loosened him up. Their mutual attention to detail allowed them to connect and establish a flow that lasted the rest of the evening.

"Guess I need to find a new frame," Jason laughed.

Stephanie gave him a half-hearted laugh and excused herself to the bathroom. She really did love Jason. What was she thinking? Jason was a good husband. He never did anything to deserve what she was doing to him. Never would he do to her what she was doing to him. She decided right then that she needed to end things with Kenneth. While it felt good to be admired, it was crossing lines that shouldn't be crossed. She had something good here; her kids were part of this gift, and it wasn't worth losing it all for a flirt and a smile.

That night Stephanie and Jason made love, like old times. She wasn't sure if it was finding the menu, but something sparked inside Jason, and he gave himself to her. The passion they shared felt like they were newlyweds again. She felt loved. She felt desired. The thought of another man melted away with every caress. Every kiss took her deeper into what she needed from her husband. Stephanie was looking for compassion, and Jason met every need without a word.

Friday, November 21, 2025

"Good morning, my lovely lady," Jason said, pouring himself a cup of coffee. He grabbed her from behind with his free hand, kissing the nape of her neck.

"Good morning, yourself." Stephanie glowed.

"The kids up yet?" he asked.

"Yes," she giggled, brushing him off, "So don't get any bright ideas."

"Darn it." He let go and sat at the kitchen table.

"What got into you last night?" she asked but didn't want to sound ungrateful.

"I guess seeing the menu reminded me of us back then. It's been so long since we've just let go and been together. We both have been so preoccupied with work, and I miss you."

Those were words she had longed to hear for a while. But was it in time? "I miss you too, Jase." Of course, it was. She smiled again, thinking of the night before.

"What does your day look like?" Jason asked.

Remembering she left her team hanging the day before, she had deadlines to ensure were made. "I have to head in early. I need to make sure Vanessa sent off our client work, and if not, I have to send out emails explaining why we missed our deadlines," she gritted her teeth. "Vanessa's good, so I shouldn't have anything to worry about. But…"

"Trust but verify," Jason said.

"Exactly," Stephanie said, her finger pointed. "You get it."

"Yep," Jason nodded. "You go get 'em. I have to chase a few AC installers."

"Should be an early day, though," she said, looking at the clock. "We're caught up, and it's Friday. We actually may have a free weekend. But I haven't checked my email yet."

Jason laughed. "Well, now you've gone and done it."

"What, jinxed myself? Naw, you know I don't believe in that. Not conducive to my writing style."

"Well, it's all about my style. So, hush it, woman."

Now it was Stephanie's turn to laugh. "I need to get dressed and check on the munchkins upstairs. Need to get them off to school."

The traffic was lighter than usual, and Stephanie was grateful. She just wanted to get through work and on to her weekend. It had been a while since she'd had an entire weekend off. And being able to rest would be a welcome change. If Vanessa accomplished everything, the office should be empty. With all assignments submitted, the staff would be free to pursue their weekend plans. So, the more work they did, the shorter time she would spend there.

When she pulled into the lot, it was relatively full. Their office was not the only one that shared the parking lot, so it was difficult to determine whether her staff was still around. She wasn't in any mood to visually check cars, so she entered the four-story building, and took the elevator to the top floor, where their offices overlooked the highway. When the elevator binged, she looked down the hall. Everything was relatively quiet—no music or other voices, which was a good sign. She pulled out her electronic key and swiped it at the door. It clicked and she turned the knob.

The office was dark, the main lights were off, and it seemed the main room was deserted. She released a relaxed sigh. All work had been submitted, and there would be no aggravated emails when she turned on her computer. She did smell fresh coffee, however. This alerted her to the possibility of someone being in an office. Then it hit her. Only one person would come in on a day of—Kenneth. She stopped in her tracks and almost turned around. But the door shut behind her, making a loud *clank* that would've alerted anyone to her presence.

"That you, boss?" a distant voice called.

Too late.

"Yeah, just came in to check on things," Stephanie answered to the darkness. "I shouldn't be long here. Just need to check email, and I'll be out of here."

Kenneth came out of his office. He was in jeans and an untucked white button-up shirt. He looked amazing.

"No need to rush off. I am just wrapping up a piece for next week. I will be out of town on Monday and Tuesday, so I need to finish it today."

"Out of town?"

"Yeah, you remember; I'm heading to the coast for some R'n'R?" He smiled with a wink.

She practically melted.

"Yes, I remember now." Stephanie remembered them talking about it over one of their meals. He had asked her to go. She rejected his offer for obvious reasons.

"Still not too late to change your mind," Kenneth said.

"You know I can't. I explained this to you. Please don't ask again," she said firmly, but standing before him made it difficult to say no. She tried to think back to the night before with Jason for strength, but with this man standing before her, she felt her resolve starting to weaken.

Kenneth nodded. "I'm sorry. Just thought I would ask one last time. Just in case you had second thoughts. I'm here for you; you know that, right?"

"Yes, I know. Thank you."

"Well, I need to get back to this article," Kenneth said, pointing toward his office. "If I don't see you before you leave, have a great weekend." He left with a rakish wink.

Stephanie reached her private office and shut the door,

kicking herself for entertaining some lascivious thoughts. *Stop doing that,* she chided herself. When she finally gathered herself, she turned on her computer and went through her inbox. There weren't any new assignments from prospective clients, just thank yous and kudos from existing clients and payment confirmations from work submitted.

Stephanie opened the company account file, checked the balances, and glowed at what she had grown the company into. It was far above anything she had dreamed. She made a few clicks, paid each of her writers, and imagined the looks on their faces when their paychecks arrived. Now she could finally get on with their weekends.

As she paused from her task, she imagined Kenneth's smile again. As if on cue, there was a knock on the door. With a reservation, she responded, "Come in."

"Hey, boss," Kenneth said, entering the room. "I was wondering if I could possibly go ahead and get paid for the piece I'm completing now. I know it's early and not part of this pay period, but I could use the funds for this trip."

Thinking about the abundance in the account and the brief Kenneth was writing was for a long-term client, Stephanie nodded. "I don't see an issue with it, Kenneth. But this will be the only time I can do this. I don't want this to become a habit, nor do I want others to think this is an okay thing to do."

"Thank you, Mrs. Marshall," Kenneth said, extending his hand for a handshake.

Stephanie stood and walked around her desk to shake his hand. This was her first mistake. She accepted his hand and held it for a bit too long. That was her second mistake. Her eyes met his and locked. Mistake number three.

Then, it happened. He pulled her in, and she allowed it. Their lips met. She felt powerless to stop herself. When he released their passionate kiss, he asked again. "You sure you can't get away for just one night?"

"I will see what I can do," Stephanie said. And she meant it.

Chapter
Five

Friday, November 21, 2025

"Y ou sure got a bounce in your step, buddy," Blake said. "You must've gotten lucky last night."

Jason didn't respond. He continued to beam and whistle while looking over the plans on his drafting table.

"*Ahhhh,*" Blake said. "Who's the lucky lady?"

"Seriously?" Jason said. "Stephanie. My wife."

"Really? Well, I wouldn't know. In the few years I've known you, you rarely talk about her, much less about getting lucky with her."

"I keep those things private. She's my wife."

"Suit yourself. So, things got hot and heavy then?" Blake nudged.

"Let's just say we had a pleasant evening together," Jason said.

"Have you made your morning after call yet?"

Jason gave a blank stare.

"How long have you been married?"

"Almost eight years," Jason said.

"Well, you should know this one. The morning after call. The one that tells her you're still thinking about her. Women love that. I learned that the hard way. My wife schooled me on that early on. We have a great date together, and if I don't call her the next morning to remind her that I had a good time, I may as well not take her out in the first place."

"Really?"

"Yeah. Call her. Tell her you're thinking of her and can't stop thinking about last night."

"Well, I *can't* stop thinking about last night."

"Right. But women need to hear that. It shows you care. One phone call goes a long way. And you've been whistling and dancing around this draft room all afternoon. You've pissed away half the morning. She probably thinks you've forgotten about her."

"Guess I better get on the phone then." Jason went into his office and dialed Stephanie's number. After three rings, it went to voice mail. He tried again, with the same result. *She's probably in a meeting or on the phone with a client*, he reasoned. She wouldn't purposely ignore his calls, especially after last night's intense evening.

Jason returned to the draft room office. Blake looked to him with eager eyes. "Well, what did she say?"

"No answer. She must be in a meeting," Jason shrugged.

"Did you leave a voicemail?"

"No," Jason said.

"Oh. Alright," Blake said. "Well, that is the next best thing—an 'I'm thinking of you' message."

"Let me guess—another Mrs. Blake idea?"

"You know it," Blake beamed.

After touring the homesite and a quick lunch, Jason tried twice more, with the same results. Three rings, then to voicemail. This was becoming an all-too-common occurrence. He felt neglected, and after last night, he thought things were on the mend. They shared a wonderful memory *and* each other. How could that be forgotten in just a few hours?

Jason shook it off. He was just being paranoid and had nothing to worry about. He knew staff meetings lasted longer when they were under deadlines. They had been running into evening hours lately. Late staff dinners were even on the menu when a client demanded a revision at the last minute. But she was a writing genius and maker of the big bucks. She was the one who enabled him to rise to his position of recognition. Many of his bigger clients would not have happened if it hadn't been for her advertising and copywriting skills. His business had been blessed through her abilities. He just needed to trust her and allow her to call him when she was available.

He might quip with Blake, but he did envy the guy's relationship with his wife. When she dropped him off in the morning, she always kissed him and ensured he had his lunch. Their affection made him smile. He thought for a moment.

I don't remember when the last time I gave even a passing thought to giving Stephanie a serious hello or goodbye kiss—or vice versa for that matter. A quick peck on the cheek now and again, but no genuine display of affection anymore. Maybe that's why last night seemed so extraordinary.

Jason realized it wasn't all on her. He was wrapped up in his career too. Delays in building materials and trying to meet deadlines kept him on job sites way past quitting time. He promised to be home earlier the next day, but there always seemed to be some snafu that got in the way. By the time he got home he had little energy left to expend on the kids or his wife. No wonder there didn't seem to be any passion in their relationship—they were both too tired to even lift their lips to meet each other.

Jason rubbed the back of his neck trying to alleviate the antsy feeling of unanswered questions. His stomach churned as this thoughts wavered between *everything's okay* and *there is definitely something wrong*. He paced the room, each step growing more intense. After calling the Alito jobsite which still hadn't heard from the AC installer, Jason needed to get out of the office. Picking up a clipboard, he decided to take a job site tour, although he had just done that an hour ago. It was nearing four o'clock, and he still hadn't heard from Stephanie. While it was not uncommon for them go the whole day without speaking to each other, it was quite unusual for her not to return his calls.

He looked at his phone for the seventieth time as he walked through the job site. Nothing. The noise of hammers and saws filled his ears. It was a welcome sound from the buzzing silence of his office. Blake was pointing at a pair of joists, and the site foreman was shaking his head. Part of Jason hoped that it wasn't a sign of a problem. Another part hoped it was. At this point, a problem to focus on would be welcome. He walked over to the conversation.

"How are we doing, gentlemen?" Jason asked.

"I don't think these beams were treated to our spec," Blake said.

Jason looked up, squinting, and walked the length of the beam. As Blake assessed, the two beams that had been installed were not coated with the fire treatment as the homeowner had purchased.

"C'mon, Damion. We discussed this last week. All beams in the roof need to be fire treated, no exceptions. Where are the beams we ordered?"

Damion shrugged. "I don't know, boss. The truck with the beams arrived yesterday. They dropped them over there. I'm just installing what we received."

Jason followed Damion to the stack of lumber and waved Blake over. Sure enough, the pallet of beams Damion was installing was labeled fire safe. Jason ran his hand over the wood and smelled his hand. Nothing. "Can you believe this?"

Blake did the same, and his reaction matched Jason's. "Well, this will set us back at least a week. I'll go call the company."

"I'm sorry, Mr. Marshall. I just figured they had a new material that was improved. I should've known better. We've been doing this long enough to recognize when something isn't right. We should stop what we are doing and ask questions before getting too involved and making things worse."

"It's not your fault, Damion," Jason said. He looked to Blake. "You got this?"

"Yeah," Blake said.

"I gotta go. Give me a call with an update on when the right wood will arrive."

"Not a problem."

Jason wasn't sure if it was a sign from on high, but he knew one thing—what Damion said made a lot of sense. Something wasn't right, and he needed to figure out what was wrong. Even if his world was about to crash in front of him, he had to know. And if everything was okay, he would know that too and have the opportunity to start mending things. But he had to see; he had to know.

Chapter
Six

Friday, November 21, 2025

It was after three o'clock, well past the time she had told Jason she would be home. Her phone had buzzed three times already. She had let it go to voicemail twice. The third, she swiped right. She knew she would have to explain that one. Kenneth had left the office shortly after their kiss. He had gone home to pack, saying he'd be back at five, and they would leave. She sat in her office lost in thought, somewhere in between agony and ecstasy.

She had crossed the line, a line she was not sure she could come back from. She sighed and shut down her computer. She picked up her phone and dialed. "Hey Jason," she said when he answered. "Sorry. Just putting out a fire here…. No, nothing that bad, just a few things that weren't finished and an unhappy client…. Yeah. It got fixed. Sorry I didn't pick up. Was on the line with the client, and then I was lost in work and just forgot to call you back. I'm sorry, love. I am heading out the door now…. Yeah, me too. See you soon."

Stephanie leaned back in her chair and exhaled. The blatant lie that roiled in her chest worked its way down to her stomach and churned there as she realized she had to go home first. She stood and walked to her office window, looking at the passing traffic. So many people were coming and going, oblivious to what she was going through. What was she going to do? She looked back at her phone, then to her office door. She had a decision to make, and since life was half about being as happy as you can make yourself, she chose to throw caution to the wind. Jason made her happy, but Kenneth made her feel wanted. And she had to explore that option. She just had to get home and grab a few things.

Stephanie swallowed hard when she saw Jason's truck in the driveway. She thought this would be a quick grab-and-dash. Now she would have to face the man she was about to lie to. Either way, she had a plan. Over the phone or face to face, it had to be done. She parked her car, and by the warmth and engine pings of his truck, she could tell he had just arrived himself. Perhaps ignoring his calls caused more of a reaction than she expected. But now it was time to put her plan into action. She drew a breath and walked through the door.

The house was silent when she entered.

"Jason?" Stephanie called out.

He didn't reply.

Does he know? Is he waiting to confront me about what I'm about to do?

"Jase? Where are you?" Stephanie didn't see him in the kitchen or living room. The refrigerator cycled on, causing her to jump. She clenched her chest and shook her head.

The sound of a toilet flush came from upstairs. Stephanie rolled her eyes. She took another breath and headed upstairs, replaying her excuse in her mind.

"Jason?" she spoke to the running water as she climbed the stairs.

"Hey, Steph. I thought I heard you pull up," he smiled as he turned and kissed her on the cheek.

"Yeah. I'm back. But not for long." Stephanie handed him a towel to dry his hands.

"Thanks." His brows furrowed. "Where are you headed?"

"One of our clients is upset we were late submitting our article. It missed their printing release, and they are *not* happy campers. So, they're threatening to cancel our contract."

"Can they do that?"

"We failed to live up to our end of it. Unfortunately, they can. You know how it is with not performing as expected."

Jason nodded.

"To prevent them from taking the weekend to think about it and having their minds made up Monday morning, I'm going down there in person to convince them we are serious about their business and to remain our clients. I figure a face-to-face meeting would be better than a phone call, or worse, an impersonal email."

"That's true. Seeing you in person will mean more. Show them you are serious about their business."

"They are my oldest client, Jase. I have to go. They're in Wilmington, on the coast. I—"

"Steph, relax," Jason said. "Go. No one's stopping you."

"Sorry. Thank you." Stephanie realized she was taking things too far and getting defensive. She relaxed her shoulders and headed into the closet for a suitcase.

Lying to Jason was easier than she thought it would be. With the three-hour drive, she said she might stay in Wilmington and get a hotel room rather than try to drive back and risk having an accident. Jason agreed.

She blamed Kenneth for the foul-up to push attention away from him rather than draw attention to him.

Jason remained in the room.

Stephanie vented to the clothes and suitcase as she spoke. She thought she would be fine if she didn't have to make eye contact with her husband.

Jason said he would keep his eye on the kids and pray for her safe return.

That last phrase caused her a pang of guilt, but she was sure she would get over it as she pulled out of the driveway.

Once on the road and headed back to the office, she hoped the pins and needles were the result of her anticipation of spending time with someone new, like the butterflies of the first date, rather than telltale signs of guilt. It was hard to tell. She hadn't felt them in a long time.

She and Kenneth had decided to meet at the office, then drive back to his place to drop off his car. They would drive hers to Wilmington, just in case Jason decided to check the mileage. If they took his car and Jason didn't see the 400 miles added to her vehicle, he might ask questions.

Not that he'd check, Stephanie mused, *but I need to have that base covered.*

Kenneth insisted on driving, and while Stephanie was apprehensive, she did find it a turn-on, seeing him drive her vehicle.

They also agreed to have two rooms down at the coast: Adjoining, but two rooms—just in case. *Better safe than sorry,* she thought.

She wasn't sure how that made her feel, but the last thing she needed was Jason driving down to be the knight in shining armor suddenly. She needed somewhere for Kenneth to run to. The thought of shoving him into the closet like an old sitcom routine made her giggle ruefully. While it sounded like a well-thought-out plan, in a way, it also made her feel cheap and dirty.

On the other hand, it also made the whole adventure feel safer. She could let herself go without the worry of getting caught.

Stephanie was still a couple of blocks from the office when she stopped at a light. Moments later, a horn sounded, pulling her from her daze. The light had changed, and she hadn't noticed. She shook off her thoughts and drove through the intersection, waving her hand at the rearview mirror in apology. Her mixed emotions had her disconnected and confused. Every inch brought her closer to the moment of no return. One minute she was sure of what to do, the next, she was afraid of the next step.

Stephanie pulled into the lot behind Kenneth's silver BMW. He had changed into blue jeans and a buttoned-up teal shirt. He was leaning on the trunk but stood when she pulled up and rolled down her passenger side window.

Leaning in, he said, "You ready, boss?"

"Okay, for the next forty-eight hours, that title better be lost from your vernacular, sir," Stephanie said with a laugh.

"Riiiiight," he said. "I will call you whatever you wish." He winked at her. "Just follow me."

If only he knew what that did to her. "Lead the way."

Kenneth signaled and revved his engine, then led her through the city. The tall multistory complex was on the edge of downtown. It was in a nice neighborhood and probably double what she figured he could afford based on what she was paying him. *He definitely does more than write for us,* she mused. *Kenneth is good at what he does. He likely has a side hustle.* His mysterious nature made him all the more alluring.

Once in front of the building, Kenneth stopped and waved for her to pull alongside him. When she did, he pointed to a striped area. "Pull up next to the entrance. I just need to grab my things, and I'll meet you over there. Remember, I'm driving."

"Okay. See you in a bit," Stephanie said. She pulled up to the front of the building and parked in an area marked for deliveries only.

Her heart raced as she waited. A grey van with a blue smile pulled up, her face matched it. She made sure to give it parking room. She didn't need an angry building manager scolding her to move. Stephanie watched the driver through her side mirror load up a hand truck with packages, curious what was in each. She imagined clothing, jewelry, and electronics. A knock on the passenger window snapped her out of her online shopping daze.

Stephanie unlocked the passenger door, and Kenneth ducked his head in. "You said I could drive."

"I know. You can take over when I stop to get gas. Get in."

"Trunk?" he said, lifting his bags.

"Oh, yeah," she said, releasing the latch.

Kenneth eased into the passenger seat with a comfortable, "*Oof.*" Then his cologne hit her. The one she had struggled to wash off the night before. The one she had trouble getting out of her dreams. But for the next forty-eight hours, she could allow herself to get lost in it. She breathed it in and put her car into drive, leaving the guy with the smiling van to hand out his mystery packages and deliver joy to their recipients.

Jason returned to the office even more confused than when he headed out. What was this sudden rush to this client? And why did she need to go tonight? Couldn't she leave in the morning and meet with them at lunch? But somewhere between her hurriedness and his fear of accusing her of doing something she wasn't, he failed to bring up the situation and let her leave. He was comfortable with her reasoning. Now he was driving back to the job site with a sick feeling and didn't know what to do about it. He could be losing his wife and wasn't bold enough to take a stand for her. If that were the case, maybe he deserved to lose her.

By the time he arrived back at the home with the failed roofing, Blake had already talked to the shipping company. Sure enough, another homeowner in Tallahassee had his lumber. They were up in arms because the contractor wanted to up their fees because they realized what they had. With Blake's mad negotiating skills, he was able to talk to two shipping companies and get both pallets of wood swapped by Monday. They would only miss the homeowner's deadline by a day.

Jason gave a wry smile and shrugged. He should've known that Blake already had the situation handled.

"There's nothing more to do here," Blake said. "We can cover it up and take a break until Monday. The boys won't like it because they don't get paid. But what can we do, right?"

"Do you have cash on you?" Jason asked.

Blake shrugged. "Always. A couple hundred, why?"

"Because we're going to treat our boys," Jason replied. "They deserve it, and it's not their fault they have two days off. Plus, we're getting close to Thanksgiving."

The two bosses pooled their money, gave their four guys a pre-holiday bonus, and sent them home to their families or their single pads with a smile.

"God has blessed us this year," Jason explained. "No reason we can't pass it on, Blake."

As expected, Kenneth offered to pay for gas at the first stop, but she reminded him she had to pay for her portion of everything to avoid suspicion. This primarily dealt with gas and the hotel room. He relented and agreed not to bring the subject up again because mentioning it only brought up the taboo, and she didn't need it on her conscience.

The drive was quiet for a few miles. Stephanie realized she had never been a passenger in her own vehicle before, and she had owned it for three years. She didn't know what to do. She wished she had the radio on when he got in; she had turned it off to hear him at his apartment and never turned it back on. Now it seemed awkward to reach over and turn it on. They had discussed which highway they'd take and the city they were heading to, but that was it. Now they sat in silence.

Was he as confused as she was? It wasn't like her to be at a loss for words. She was a writer; words were her thing. Stephanie looked around the car. The dash had a thin layer of dust on it. Not bad, only she would noticed, but she thought about the last time she washed it.

She looked out the window.

She looked at the steering wheel.

She looked at Kenneth's hands. She bit her lower lip thinking about how sexy a man's hands looked upon a steering wheel.

That made her realize she hadn't been in a car with a man in a while. She and Jason rarely went anywhere together anymore; if they did, they usually met somewhere after work in separate vehicles.

Her eyes must've rested too long upon his hands, or drool must've formed on the corner of her mouth because Kenneth spoke.

"Everything okay?"

"Yeah, sorry. Just lost in thought." Probably the wrong words. Now he'd ask what she was thinking.

"Penny for those thoughts."

"Heh. My thoughts are worth at least a quarter," Stephanie jested.

"Bill me," Kenneth said, glancing at her before returning his eyes to the road.

"Just thinking that I've never sat in the passenger seat of my car before, that's all. Thinking about how long it's been since I have ever been driven someplace."

"How long has it been?"

"Too long."

"Sorry," Kenneth said. "It shouldn't be that way. You should be taken away more often. You deserve it."

"Oh, it's not so much as not being taken. It's not having the time. Life gets so busy that it's overwhelming, and there is no opportunity for getting away."

"Nuh-uh. I don't buy it. For you, I would make time. You see here, we're on our way somewhere. Time has been made.

Nothing has gotten in the way." Kenneth reached out, took her hand, and kissed it.

Stephanie smiled and allowed her hand to be held for most of the trip. She also let go of her nervousness and turned on the radio. She learned their taste in music was not the same. *Well, you can't win them all.* Kenneth paired his phone and music app to the car. While she wasn't much of a fan of jazz, she did appreciate that he was and enjoyed several songs on his playlist.

Chapter
Seven

Friday, November 21, 2025

It was nearly ten o'clock when they pulled into the hotel's parking lot. Stephanie could smell the ocean when she opened the passenger door. She hadn't smelled that fragrance since the day she and Jason came down for a quick getaway after Evelyn was born. Her parents took the kids so they could recuperate from the late nights of being in the hospital after Evelyn developed jaundice from being born prematurely. They had to rush back to the hospital and stay an extra week. But they were told it was quite common, and a couple of weeks later, they were home with her, and all was well.

Yet a month later, the two of them were still taking turns, split-shifting, making sure she would be okay at home. Both their parents and her pediatrician said they were overdoing it and that Evie would be fine, but the worrisome parents took every precaution to ensure their angel would make it through every night.

"You okay?" the voice asked, pulling her back to reality.

Stephanie turned, and Kenneth had their bags in his hand. She shook the memory off. "Yeah, I'm fine. Sorry, just taking it all in." Stephanie pointed toward the highway and the Atlantic behind it. "You can hear the ocean if you listen."

He shrugged. "All I hear is the sound of the traffic passing. Come on, let's get inside."

He handed Stephanie her bag and nodded toward the building, "We should check in. It's getting late."

"Is there somewhere we can go to eat around here? I'm kinda hungry?" Stephanie said. She wasn't sure of his immediate intentions but didn't want the only reason to come here to be a secret rendezvous. If there was going to be an affair, he would have to earn it.

"Uh, yeah, sure. There may be a place or two along the boardwalk still open. We can ask the hotel clerk."

"Oooohh, a boardwalk. I like the sound of that," Stephanie said with a wink.

Her comment seemed to grab his attention and divert his mind from any immediate intentions. Kenneth's smile returned. "Let's check in and see what they recommend." He crooked his arm, she took his elbow, and they walked toward the hotel. But as they rounded the corner Stephanie stopped short, breaking their embrace.

"Maybe we should check in separately. Just to be safe."

"If that would make you feel more comfortable," Kenneth said. He waved toward the entrance, allowing her to go first.

"You first. I need to visit the restroom anyway. Then we can meet up after we are in our rooms. That boardwalk idea sounds fabulous."

"Sounds like a plan," Kenneth said and entered the hotel alone.

Stephanie followed after a moment and found the restroom. When she thought she had taken enough time, she exited, but Kenneth was still registering. She didn't want to approach the desk until he left so she walked through the lobby. She saw a restaurant with a few lingering patrons, but she could tell they were closing. Perhaps she could at least grab a cup of coffee.

The attached restaurant resembled an old diner but with a modern 21st century. There was a counter with circular stools. One of the patrons sat at the far end of the counter. He was nursing a cup she assumed was coffee, with the creamer decanter and packets of sugar in front of it. The man had a familiar air to him. He wore a coat and had a head of white hair. On the counter sat a tweed hat, the same color as his coat. Stephanie almost lost her footing when she realized who she was looking at. It was the man who had given her the lost menu.

"So, are you going to stare at me all night, Stephanie, or will you sit and enjoy a cup of coffee with me?" Carter said, looking up at her.

She didn't wait for a second invitation. Stephanie entered the restaurant and sat next to the stranger. "Are you following me?"

"What makes you think I'm following you?" Carter said.

"First the coffee shop, now here? What else am I supposed to think, Carter?"

"Ah, you do remember me, then? That's good. It will save me the trouble of reintroducing myself."

"I am a writer. It is my job to remember things," Stephanie explained. "You didn't answer my question."

"Am I following you? That I can answer with an honest no. I am not following you. Per se," Carter said.

"Okay," Stephanie said, confused by his vague answer.

"Did your husband enjoy what I left for the two of you?" Carter asked, sipping his coffee.

Stephanie squinted. "Where in the world did you find that menu? I know you weren't the one who stole it. Forgive me, but you just don't look like the thieving type. Did one of your relatives take it?"

"Let's just say it came into my possession, and I wanted to return it to you," Carter said.

The waitress returned and set down a cup in front of Stephanie. The aroma of hazelnut and creamer hit her senses. "Wait, how did you know?"

"The coffee shop the morning we met."

"You remember my order?"

"I remember lots of things, Stephanie," Carter said.

"Wait a minute. I never said anything about hazelnut that morning. It was a standing order. So, you couldn't know what my coffee order was."

"Fair enough. Let's just say I know things."

"Mmmhmm," Stephanie said, sipping her coffee, which was perfect. The hotel knew their stuff.

"Did you talk to the staff there?"

"Don't worry about the coffee. How I know how you take your coffee should be the least of your worries, wouldn't you agree?"

"How's that?"

Carter nodded toward the reception desk, which was now void of Kenneth.

Stephanie followed Carter's nod. The receptionist was assisting a couple. One was an obvious tourist with a floral button-up and khaki shorts.

"I'm not sure what you mean. I'm here on business, trying to keep a client from canceling business with our firm," Stephanie lied. She needed to keep the story straight. Even if this man were never to meet her husband. The possibility still existed; if the question arose, that base needed to be covered.

"We both know that's not true. We can save a lot of time by being honest with each other," Carter said with another sip of his coffee.

"Honest with each other? Okay," Stephanie started. "How did you get my husband's menu?"

"Hmm. That is a good one," Carter admitted. He nodded and took another sip. "Would you accept my answer if I said it's classified?"

"Now, who's wasting time," Stephanie said.

"Okay," Carter said. "I found it in a box."

"Who does that box belong to?"

"That I can't say."

"Can't or won't?"

"A bit of both, actually."

Stephanie sighed in defeat. "Okay. I can accept that. Protecting family, I can respect that." She sipped her coffee. "Why are you here in Wilmington?"

"That I *can* tell you. I'm here for you, Stephanie."

"For me? How's that? You don't know me. And you could've found me in Evansville at any time. In fact, you did. What more could you want? Do you have more fascinating keepsakes for me?"

"No, but I'm here to help you from losing them."

"I'm not sure I follow you."

"Your husband, Stephanie. I'm here to keep you from making the biggest mistake of your life."

"I'm not—"

"Stephanie, please don't lie to me. I know more than you know. And to prove it, I will show you how serious the situation is." Carter lifted his palm toward the ceiling, "Well, *He* is going to show you how serious it is."

"He?"

"Yes. He."

"As in God?"

"God," Carter acknowledged.

"Heh. What did they put in your coffee, Carter?"

"I'm not joking with you, Stephanie. This is a dire situation. I'm sure you are aware of this. Those pangs you've been feeling each time you thought about coming down here?"

"How do you know about those?" Stephanie's face wrinkled in disbelief.

"Those were God telling you that this was wrong," Carter said, pointing toward her chest.

"I don't believe God would behave in that way."

"Well, He would and has. Why do you think I'm here?"

"God sent you?"

"You can say that."

"What, are you an angel or something?"

Carter smiled. "You could say that."

"And you've been sent to keep me from doing something I'd regret?"

Carter pursed his lips and nodded. "Now you're getting it."

"I'm not sure I buy your story, Carter," Stephanie said, taking another sip of coffee.

"You are free to believe me or disregard what I'm telling you. Free will. I'm just the messenger sent to help you make the right decision."

"I don't suppose you could prove you're one of God's angels?"

"You're returned menu wasn't proof enough?"

Stephanie thought for a second, "Ehhh, you could've just found that on the thief who stole it."

"You have me there. But you can't expect me to make water turn to wine or fire to fall from heaven. It doesn't work that way."

"Then this could just be a coincidence, and my guilt is trying to keep me from having a wonderful evening with a man who honestly cares about me."

"If that's what you believe, Stephanie. But you must consider what you'll leave behind if you proceed down this path. Once you cross that line, there's no going back. You can't take off that weight. You thought the smell of cologne on your neck and clothes was difficult to wash off? The weight of adultery doesn't wash off. You carry that forever."

Stephanie choked on her coffee. How in the world could he know about the cologne on her clothes? No one knew about that hug but her, Kenneth, and Vanessa. *Vanessa!*

"Did Vanessa put you up to this?"

"I'm sorry, I don't know who Vanessa is," Carter said. "I'm just trying to help you, Stephanie. It's my job."

"As an angel of the Lord."

"Yes."

"Well, Mr. Carter," Stephanie said, standing.

"Mr. Jennings. Carter is my first name."

"My apologies. Mr. Jennings. If you don't have further proof, I'm about to head upstairs and enjoy the evening that I've earned. I don't know how you found me here or how you know these things about me." Stephanie drained the remainder of her cup then waved her finger at Carter. "You almost had me, and I don't know what Vanessa or anyone else told you, but Kenneth cares about me, and we are about to share a memorable evening together, and *that* means something."

"I sure hope you will feel the same way in the morning," Carter said.

"I *know* I will," Stephanie said. "Nothing can change that—not you or your God."

Chapter
Eight

Tuesday, November 22, 2005
Saturday, November 22, 2025

"Missus? Missus?" Stephanie was woken by someone tapping her shoulder. She snapped up to see a confused cleaning lady with a bottle of Windex in her hand. "Missus? What are you doing in this room?"

Stephanie had to shake the heavy feeling from her head. She had never experienced a hangover in her life, but if she were to have had one, she imagined this is what it would feel like. Her head felt like a sledgehammer had hit her between her eyes, and every muscle in her body ached. She groaned as she tried to stand; that wasn't happening at the moment.

She had little memory of the night before. She did remember, however, a man in a tweed hat yelling that God was about to strike her down. She had to laugh, but even that made her ache. Maybe this is what a lightning bolt from heaven felt like. The thought made her shudder. *Ouch.*

The maid was still in her ear. "Missus? Who are you, and why are you in this room?"

"This is *my* room. I checked in last night." That much she remembered, or assumed.

"No, missus. This room is listed as vacant. What is your name?"

"Stephanie Marshall," she said, rubbing her temple. *Does she have to talk so loud?*

The maid went to the phone on the nightstand and dialed. Stephanie looked at the nightstand. It looked odd. She remembered it being white; it was now brown. *Wow, what did I drink last night? What did Kenneth give her? Oh, hell…*

Stephanie was suddenly filled with fear and wondered what Kenneth had done to her. "Where is the man I came here with?"

The maid hung up the phone. "I don't know. All I do is clean rooms, ma'am. Our clerk says they don't have any record of this room being occupied, and there is no information of a Stephanie Marshall checking in to this hotel."

"That's not possible. Let me call him back—" Stephanie reached for the phone.

"Her," the maid said, placing her hand over the phone. "Gayla Yandel is the manager. She will tell you what you need to do downstairs. But the front desk clerk says you need to vacate this room immediately. It's reserved, and I'm here to give it a final cleaning."

"I need to find the man I checked in with," Stephanie demanded. "I may have been drugged and raped. Don't you understand? I don't have any memory of last night. I arrived here with this man, and I don't have any memories since I arrived and your rude awakening. Now I need you to call your manager, call the police, call whomever you need to. I need help. Now!!"

An hour later, Stephanie was sitting in the hotel's lobby. She was trembling. This was not the lobby she had been sitting in eight hours earlier. The reception desk had a creepy cherry-wood finish, and the restaurant was missing the diner countertop where she and Carter had their spiritual discussion. *What in the world is going on?* Stephanie had already checked the address and questioned if she was at the right hotel. Even an angry outburst about their sanity didn't get far. The only thing she did have was the suitcase she brought with her on the trip; that much remained unchanged. Everything else had experienced a time warp.

The manager approached her and cleared her throat. She leaned over and as quietly as possible said, "Ms. Marshall, we can do one of two things. We can allow you to leave the premises without asking questions. I will even throw in a complimentary breakfast in our diner. Or we can call the authorities and allow them to handle the situation." She raised her eyebrows with the second option.

Stephanie knew she was in no position to fight. Either Kenneth had nothing to do with this, or he was in on it, and fighting would only make things worse. She knew she needed to get out while she was ahead.

"I will leave," Stephanie said. "I'm sorry to have troubled you. Yes, I would appreciate the meal. I promise to keep to myself."

The manager nodded, handing her the meal voucher. "We thank you for choosing our fine establishment, Ms. Marshall," the manager said, then quickly walked away.

Stephanie sighed, and before anything worse could happen, she headed into the restaurant. Her skin crawled walking into the place that was worlds different from the previous night. A sign instructed her to seat herself, so she found a booth near the window that gave her a partial view of the ocean, hoping it would calm her nerves.

A waitress came and poured her a cup of coffee. She thought of asking about hazelnut, but without the diner-looking counter, she thought better of it. Still, the coffee's aroma was pleasant and inviting. It reminded her of something she'd have at Latte Loco. She took a sip, and for the first time that morning, smiled. Coffee was a way of relaxing an anxious mind and comforting when you needed it the most.

"It's great stuff, isn't it," the familiar voice stated.

Stephanie's head spun around, and the familiar figure that matched the voice stood at a distance.

"What the—"

"Relax. Relax," Carter said, with his hands surrendered. "If you give me a moment, I will explain everything. Just please remain calm, and we can both get through this in one piece."

"I don't know about that," Stephanie said, turning her attention back to her coffee.

Carter approached the booth and lowered his voice. "For one, I want to ease your mind. This has nothing to do with Kenneth. Your honor is still intact."

Stephanie sighed. "Okay. That does make me feel better. But what happened here? Where am I?"

"I think the better question is, *when* are you?" Carter said.

They were both silent. The room clanked with dishes and the stirring of coffee cups, hushed conversations, and the mild tone of Muzak.

"May I sit?" Carter said, extending a hand. "I believe I owe you an explanation."

Stephanie nodded.

"Wonderful." Carter sat, and a waiter set down a cup and filled it with coffee. "This place has fabulous coffee. I haven't had coffee like this since I was in Houston."

"You're from Houston?"

"I'm from everywhere," Carter chuckled.

"Ah, that's right, you're an angel," Stephanie snickered, taking a sip of her coffee.

Carter looked to the ceiling. "The lady asks for a sign, and she still holds on to her disbelief."

"Oh. By all means. You have my attention, Mr. Jennings."

"Please, call me Carter. All my friends call me Carter."

"Okay—*Carter*. You have my full attention. And obviously, you intervened to prevent what you assumed to be a mistake last night. What *did* you do, by the way—drug my coffee? So, I wake up never having met up with Kenneth. Ahh, no, I get it. This is a dream. And I will wake up with an epiphany and turn my life around."

Carter reached over and pinched Stephanie's arm.

"Ouch! Hey, what did you do that for?"

"If you were sleeping, that would've awakened you," Carter said, then shrugged. "Guess you're not asleep. This is real, Stephanie."

"Okay. This is real." Stephanie rubbed her arm. "And you're here to prevent me from sleeping with Kenneth?"

"Among other things."

Stephanie sipped her coffee and looked around at the dark wood, "What other things? Why are we here? What happened in my past? What year is this anyway?"

"2005, I believe." Carter looked at his wrist, at a watch that wasn't there.

"In 2005 I was sixteen."

"That sounds about right," Carter said, then pointed at Stephanie. "You'd be in high school. That serves our purpose."

"Our purpose?"

Carter smiled and laughed. "There is a purpose for all things. He has a purpose for all He does. It will be revealed in time. But time is something we don't have, Stephanie. We must be moving."

"Moving, where?"

"Where were you right now in 2005?"

Stephanie looked around her, "My phone?!"

Carter laughed. "That is one thing that didn't travel with you. It wouldn't work here anyway. It would just be an expensive alarm clock, and you couldn't be seen with something fifteen years out of its time period, so it's best just to leave it where it came from."

"How am I supposed to—"

"You won't need it anyway. We won't be here long. Plus, who are you going to call?"

Stephanie nodded, seeing his point.

"Is my car still here? Did it make the time trip?"

Carter laughed. "You won't need your car, either. That would take too long. Time is pressing, and we need to get things done."

"So, how do we get back to Evansville?"

Carter winked. "Take my hand."

"So, what, are we going to teleport or something?"

Carter laughed. "Just take my hand. Don't worry about everyone else. We aren't really here. They won't remember a thing."

Stephanie looked into Carter's grey eyes from under his cap. They were steel and serious; they were trustworthy. Somehow, she knew she believed him. She wondered why she hadn't from the beginning.

"Okay," she said and placed her hand in his.

"Now close your eyes, and don't open them."

Stephanie obeyed, and as soon as she did, a warmth surrounded her like nothing she had ever experienced. It was as if she were wrapped in heated velvet; she relaxed into its embrace. Carter began to pray. She couldn't make out his exact words, but she did hear, *God, thank you*, and *guide*. As the comfort grew, the more distant Carter became. His voice was soothing, it aided in her relaxation. Then, just as she was about to fall asleep, a voice pulled her back to consciousness.

"Stephanie. Stephanie. We are here."

Stephanie opened her eyes and looked around. It took her a moment to realize where she was, but the smell of pizza and canned corn jarred her memory. She was at her high school, standing in line for lunch. The disorientation made her want to pass out for a moment. Once she regained her stability, the voice returned.

"Just do what you need to do here, and we can move on."

"What is that?" Stephanie said aloud.

"Pizza," said the lunch server. "Same thing we have every Friday. Now move it, you're holding up the line, Ms. Chambers."

Carter spoke again, "Only you can hear me, but I won't be here long. Do what you came to do. And when you find what you're supposed to find, we will move on. God be with you, Stephanie."

"Carter," Stephanie said. "Wait! Carter?"

"Who is Carter, Ms. Chambers? Are you okay?"

Stephanie nodded. "Yes, sorry. I'm fine." She moved through the line and tried to remember what was next. Where did she go for lunch in her sophomore year? She figured to play it safe, sit alone, and allow whomever it was to come to her.

After eating about half of her pizza, everything clicked. She recalled that she would scarf her lunch and head to the editorial office, where she wrote and edited for the school paper and looked for opportunities to write something for the community. Her sophomore year was the year she received an award for an article she wrote about homelessness in her community. It was about Thanksgiving that a story she wrote was printed. It opened the door for shelters to give more opportunities for the homeless. She dropped her pizza and ran out of the cafeteria and up the stairs to the newspaper office.

"Where have you been?" the senior editor asked.

"Sorry, I lost track of time.

"You?" the editor said and laughed. "Unprecedented."

"Relax, I'm here now. I'll have this done in no time." Stephanie was sure of it. She knew the article by heart. Even at thirty-six, she knew it. And with her age and experience, she had always wished she could go back and change a couple of things because she knew so much more. She had often commented that her innocent eyes were so foolish back then.

Stephanie pulled up the document and laughed at how long it took for the computer to load. She was used to point, click, and shoot. When the program finally opened, her adult mind in her teenage body read over the piece. Her fingers hovered over the keyboard for a moment, then she sat back in the chair. She looked at the editor and remembered how excited he was for her to be recognized for her achievement. Not that his approval mattered, but her memory swam over what happened after that. City recognition, mayoral praise, the funds were raised, and more people were fed and housed that year than had ever been in prior years.

Stephanie closed her eyes, hit save, and let the computer do its thing. Then she grabbed a thumb drive out of her desk and saved the article. She pondered, *What could I change that would make it any better? Would changing it now affect what accolades came of it? Am I even supposed to change it? No, I should leave it as it is.*

"Here you go, boss man." Stephanie handed her prized piece in. "This one will make you weep. It's the one."

"All my writers say that. Why should yours be any different, Steph," he said without even looking up. "You're a sophomore, and it's your first semester on the paper. Writers don't hit their prized pieces until the final semester of their junior year. But I appreciate your enthusiasm and tenacity."

"Ahh, I just have a feeling. I put my heart and soul into this piece. I believe you will have a light shining on you for this one. When one of us shines, we all shine. After all, we are a team here," Stephanie said, and she meant it.

Chapter
Nine

Tuesday, November 22, 2005
Saturday, November 22, 2025

Stephanie was proud of what her story grew into. Personally and economically for the community. Its success would eventually ignite her hunger for writing. But from what she remembered, it all ended up being just a High School fantasy. Life took over, and her writing aspirations took a backseat as those around her told her that writing wasn't a worthwhile career. As an impressionable teen, she believed the adults around her and turned in her keyboard. She ended up attending community college, received a degree in business administration, and was hired as an office manager for a construction company. It wasn't until that company had issues with advertising that she began to write again. The company eventually began to pay her for her work and became her first client.

Stephanie was excited about the opportunity to relive this questioning moment. Only this time, she knew what the outcome would be. But what was this uneasy feeling flowing through her? Was it the teenage part of her? She tried to assure herself that it was going to be okay about the future she would experience, but her younger mind and heart wouldn't hear it. Stephanie leaned back at her desk, wondering if things would indeed repeat as they did the first time.

Wiping a tear from her cheek, Stephanie shook the doubt away. Pride, elation, fear—it didn't matter; she was in the moment. She remembered keeping tissue packs in her desk, so she pulled the creaky steel door open. This is where she stored her personal toolkit. She kept pens, the said tissues, a couple of steno pads for when she didn't have the luxury of recording, and other odds and ends. She popped open the plastic case, and the smell of ink hit her. Not just any ordinary ink—typewriter ink. And she remembered.

Stephanie may have been a thirty-six-year-old sitting in a sixteen-year-old body, but both minds jumped into hyperdrive when she pulled out the typewriter ribbon. Its smell was distinct, as was the style. Stephanie could almost hear the Smith Corona *buzz* and the *clickety-clack* of the keys. The original had been a gift from her grandmother after she read a few poems Stephanie had penned. Her words were etched into her memories.

"An artist like this shouldn't be writing their work. You need something more apt to the art."

Her grandmother had a typewriter at her office, and on the day she spoke those words, Stephanie went back home one typing instrument heavier and with a half case of those ribbons.

Stephanie fell in love with that electronic typewriter. She, still to this day, could pick that tone out of a lineup. The odor of the warmed ink would send her into a writing zone that her teachers found difficult to pull her from. It was well worth it. That award when she was sixteen, just six months after receiving the gift, spoke volumes. Not just because it was her passion but because the subject she wrote about was her grandmother's passion—the passion for helping others.

Her grandmother had raised her after her parents passed, and pairing that with stories of those who are homeless helped life become relatable. It was about sharing a common story, but it was also about seeing that one difference that can cause each life to take a different course. Her grandmother gave her the ability to excel. "You just need to be the difference in someone else's life to allow them to experience the kind of success you do," the older woman said.

Writing was Stephanie's passion; it had always been. She wrote on that Smith Corona for over a decade, even after her marriage to Jason. But she knew its days were numbered as technology raced inexorably forward; paper and ink were passé. And her company's growth was no longer just about her. She had others under her who did the work she used to do. The warmth she now felt came from a hard drive, and the *buzz* was from the halogen lights of her office. There wasn't much passion in those things—not like that of her trusty Smith Corona.

Kenneth understood that passion. She had talked about it with him, and he understood. He shared the thrill of getting the job done. It wasn't that Jason didn't, but his version was with nails and boards; it was just different. It wasn't like building passion within someone to drive them to action. That was what words did. Words could bring people to tears or infuriate them to no end. Sometimes it could happen within the same piece. That was the beauty of it. Kenneth got that. Jason shrugged at it and went back to hammering.

Stephanie looked around the newsroom. No one was paying attention to her emotional state. She had long forgotten about the tissue. Tears fell from her cheeks and onto her T-shirt. Taking a breath, she pulled her hair back and reached into her pocket for a hair-tie, but came up empty. She thought of Jason. He would always have one handy for her. Sighing, she let go of her hair and wiped her face with her palm. She put her tote away, save the ribbon—this puzzle needed solving. She couldn't understand how it ended up in the box. It had never been in her desk when she was a teen. That typewriter stayed at home; there was no reason for that ribbon to be there. She looked at the reel intently, then at her fingers. With their dampness, purple stains had transferred onto the tissues.

Laying the ribbon on the desk, she pulled more tissue from the small wrapper. It cleaned the mess, but the stains remained.

What was it Carter said, something about the stains remaining? Was this ribbon some kind of object lesson? Was her actions with Kenneth this evident? Would Jason know? Does he already know?

Suddenly his hammering didn't matter as much. The look in her eyes when she arrived home, carrying this secret—the stain of what she had done would be evidence enough. Would it be something she could live with? She now feared losing Jason. With everything they had been through together, and that amazing night they had just shared before she chose to go on this adventure. *God, what have I done?*

The floor began to tremble, and the sun flickered through the window blinds brighter than usual. Stephanie stood. Her heart raced. The water cooler in the corner was sloshing, and books and files began to fall from desks and shelves.

Her editor sat at his desk, oblivious to the world falling apart around him. The photo of the football team's mascot fell off the wall with a crash. Stephanie screamed. It all went unnoticed.

A voice spoke, "Hold on, Stephanie. This may sting a bit."

A bright flash of light enveloped Stephanie, and the office went black, or her vision of it.

"Just close your eyes," the familiar voice said.

"Carter?" Stephanie said.

"Relax," Carter assured her.

Wherever or whatever state she was in flashed again. A queasiness overwhelmed her, and she thought she was going to be sick. A tiny pinprick of light came into view, then grew brighter.

"You need to relax, Stephanie," Carter said. "Close your eyes."

Stephanie obeyed, more because she was growing dizzy. As she relaxed the uneasiness left her. Peace and warmth filled her heart, like it had when she and Carter left the first time. She could feel his hands close around hers, and she could hear his prayers again. It concluded with, "Amen."

"Okay, we're here," Carter said in almost a whisper.

Stephanie opened her eyes. The room was bright, she had to shield her eyes from the sun glowing through the windows. Once they adjusted, she saw Carter sitting in front of her. He was sipping a cup of coffee. They were sitting in the booth in the motel diner where they had been sitting when the time-shift began.

"We're back," Stephanie said, rubbing her eyes. They ached, and she felt disoriented.

"You could say that," Carter said. He nodded to his left.

She glanced over. The coffee bar was there. The one where they had their confrontation before she had gone upstairs. They were back to their normal time. Or were they? With the sun shining, it must be the day after, or maybe the morning before?

"Okay, we're at the hotel. I can see that, but *when* are we?" Stephanie asked, realizing it was perhaps best not to assume.

"Just a stopping point. No need to be concerned about that right now."

"Stopping point? You mean there's more? Carter, what just happened?"

"You tell me. I'm just the vehicle," Carter said, leaning back in the booth.

"What vehicle? Who sent you?"

"We've already been through that."

"Right. God sent you," Stephanie said, folding her arms.

"Why is that so hard to believe? You've already seen the proof," Carter said.

"I just find it difficult to believe. God left me alone a long time ago when He allowed my parents to die in that car accident," Stephanie said a bit too loudly. It drew looks from a couple at a nearby table. She waved in apology, then turned back to Carter. "My parents never got to see me get married, never met their grandkids, never saw me win one award."

"But you do have the love of others around you. You have proof of that now. You have a little reminder of that love."

"The menu?"

"Among other things," Carter nodded at her hoodie.

Stephanie didn't realize it, but she put her hand into her front pocket and pulled the item out; it was her typewriter ribbon.

"But how?" Stephanie muttered, mouth agape. "It was just …"

"… a dream?"

Stephanie didn't answer. She just stared at the ribbon, then at her ink-stained fingers.

"It is God, Stephanie. He wants to show that He loves you and has always been there. He brought people into your life to inspire you. Even when bad things happen, good things can come out of it."

"My parents," Stephanie said.

"Yes. Let me ask you something," Carter said. "Who was your biggest inspiration that got you started as a writer?"

Stephanie swallowed, and in a near whisper, she answered, "My grandmother."

"Exactly," Carter said. "Now, I'm not saying that your parents died so you could become a writer. I *am* saying that God uses events in people's lives to direct them along the path that is their calling. Their deaths made you stronger, and your writing ability results from what you've been through."

Stephanie stared at the typewriter ribbon. She clenched it and remembered her grandmother's quote. She felt her emotions building again.

"I'm sorry for your loss," Carter said. "She was a lovely lady."

"You knew her?"

"No, not personally, but I read up on all my assignments and get to know them before I make my first approach. I heard about her and how much she loved you and devoted her life to you. She was a good Christian woman. She was always in prayer for you."

"I know. She told me often enough," Stephanie admitted. "That's one of the reasons it pains me to think about her. I feel like I've let her down."

"Nonsense. Look at how successful you've become. Got married, raised two beautiful children..."

Stephanie chuckled. "She always had a good story to tell."

"Yes, and I do love a good story," Carter said, leaning in. "We all have a story to tell, Stephanie. Happy stories, sad stories, true stories, made-up stories, anything and everything. Life isn't life without a good story. I have a story; You have a story. Your grandmother had one. It's what makes us who we are. And we need to tell people those stories. Without our stories," Carter pointed to the TV screen playing, "we're just yesterday's news."

Stephanie looked at the screen. The Weather Channel was showing the forecast—clear and seventy-five degrees.

"You know, it's never too late."

Stephanie sighed. "It's not that easy, Carter."

"Still not convinced?"

Stephanie turned her attention outside where she could see people walking toward the beach. She had almost forgotten where she was. How could she seek God in a place like this, her secret rendezvous?

"Not yet," Stephanie said.

Carter looked to the ceiling.

"Hear that, Gabe; she's still not convinced."

Carter shrugged. "Come on. Let's go for a walk. I need some fresh air."

"Where are we going?"

"I hear there is a place over on the Boardwalk that serves the best gelato. You ever had it?"

"Gelato?" Stephanie said. "No, never heard of it."

"Hmm. That's what the waitress said. I tried it once in Houston and fell in love. Now I have a hankering for it." Carter stood and waved her on.

Stephanie picked up her ribbon, put it in her pocket, and looked around them. "Where are my things?"

"They've been taken care of. Don't worry," Carter said. "We have things to do."

"Why don't I like the sound of that?" Stephanie said. She stood and followed Carter out of the restaurant.

Chapter
Ten

Saturday, November 22, 2025

The day felt warmer than seventy-five, but Stephanie wasn't paying as much attention to the temperature as she was to where Carter was leading her. His hair was much brighter than it seemed indoors. She almost needed to shield her eyes, it was so bright white. And that was just the part peeking from under the cap.

From the hotel entrance a path led them to the place Kenneth had briefly mentioned the night before. She didn't realize it was actually called "The Boardwalk," nor did she expect the small amusement park there. Now it made sense that Carter would find an odd snack she hadn't heard of before.

Gelato, did he call it?

"It's just through here, I believe," Carter said, pointing. He was like a child on a mission to be the first in line for a ride.

"Gelato?"

"Gelato," Carter affirmed. "My source said there would be a giant sign."

"Giant and neon, I suppose," Stephanie tried to reassure.

"That would be helpful."

Stephanie couldn't help but laugh. "You mean to tell me that God doesn't have this stuff at a buffet table up in Heaven?"

Now it was Carter's turn to laugh. "I'm not that type of angel."

"So, what type of angel are you then? Fallen?"

Carter cringed. "Heaven's no."

"So, you didn't do something wrong and need to work your way back?"

"I choose to be here. It allows me to help people and guide them back to God."

"And I'm your current assignment?"

"There it is!" Carter exclaimed, pointing to the location with a giant cup of frozen yogurt in the window.

Stephanie followed Carter, who was now not so heavenly, as he made his way through a couple of groups to the beacon that had called to him. He found the *Order Here* window and, within moments, had a cup in one hand and two spoons in the other. Stephanie stayed back and allowed him to return to her. "You didn't want anything?"

"I'm fine," Stephanie said, having to laugh at the display in front of her. "Wouldn't this be considered gluttony?"

"Oh, I hope not," Carter said, taking another spoonful. "You know. Each place I've tried has its own… pizazz… on what it tastes like. I mean, this is just plain vanilla. But I kid you not, I taste cinnamon." Carter extended the spoon. "Here, try it."

Stephanie extended her hand, pushing his favor away, laughing. "I'm fine, Carter. I trust you. It's good."

"You don't know what you're missing." Carter took another bite, closing his eyes in delight. "Isn't the writer in you the least bit intrigued about my insatiable interest in gelato?

Wouldn't that be part of your job description?" Carter said, scooping a generous spoonful off his mound of vanilla.

She was a bit curious, and for a moment the confection did look appealing. Carter spotted it immediately.

"See," he pointed at her with his spoon. "Here." He handed her the second spoon he held. "You must try this. I kid you not, there is cinnamon in this."

Stephanie laughed as she took a small spoonful.

"No," Carter said. "You need a bigger bite than that. Come on, Stephanie, as a journalist you need the full effect."

Stephanie nodded, took a heaping spoonful, and ate it. She had to admit it was delicious, and there *was* a hint of cinnamon.

"Good?" Carter asked.

"It's tasty."

"See, I told you." Carter smiled and took his next bite.

Stephanie smiled, then breathed deeply. "Okay. So, you are here on a mission for me." She looked back at the hotel behind her. "I guess you've succeeded. If today *is* Saturday, then last night is over. God—and I suppose you—know where Kenneth is. I am safe from making the mistake that was going to happen."

Carter nodded, then finished his last bite.

"Was that vision supposed to remind me of my past success? Speaking of, how did that ribbon get in my desk? I never took it to the school. After the award, my grandmother talked about her award for writing. She said she took the ribbon out of her typewriter as a keepsake. I felt it was symbolic, so I replaced the ribbon in *my* Smith Corona. I put it in a memento box, *at home*. It was *never* at the school or in my toolbox there. After Jason and I were married, that box, among other keepsakes, ended up in storage."

"Maybe the same thief that broke into your husband's office, perhaps?" Carter raised his eyebrows.

Stephanie squinted. "You see? That right there. It's remarks like that, Carter. They cast a shadow of doubt on your story. You have to remember; I conduct research for a living. My stories have to pass a thorough inspection, or I lose all credibility. I lose my credibility, and I'm out of a job."

"I see," Carter said, stroking his thick stubble.

"So, when you even hint that you stole both items, it makes sense," Stephanie said, sitting back in her chair.

"What does your keen research ability say about this slick pickpocket's ability to place that stolen item in a past dream of yours that you brought here through a portal in time?"

Stephanie could only stare. "I can't answer that. Yet." She took a breath. "But I will. Give me time."

They sat in silence for a moment, both in thought.

"You like the ocean?" Carter finally said.

"Yeah, it's wet," Stephanie said with a shrug.

"Let's continue our walk. They say the sand is different here than in Texas. I'd like to see it."

"So, you visited the beach when you lived in Houston?"

"Once or twice."

"How far have you been, Carter?"

"Let's walk, and I'll tell you about it," Carter said again with a neck wave.

Stephanie nodded. She took a final glance at the hotel and then at the parking lot. She hoped her car would still be there when they returned. She knew she would have a lot of explaining to do when she got home and not just to Jason. Then it occurred to her; she came in the same car with Kenneth.

"Carter. I need to go back to the hotel and see what happened to my car. I need to check on Kenneth. I have to—"

Carter interrupted, "I can assure you that all your concerns have been addressed."

"But…" Stephanie stopped short. Carter walked around her and stood in her path.

"Stephanie. Please. Look in my eyes." Carter lifted his hat, and his clear grey eyes took hold of her again. They were honest and assured her there was nothing to be concerned about. What she left behind at that hotel didn't matter compared to what was happening right now. "Everything is going to be okay. Let it go."

"Okay, Carter," Stephanie said. "Let's go. I'm right behind you."

"Great," Carter said, extending his hand toward the beach. "I need to work off that gelato. Not as much fat as ice cream, but it doesn't mean there is none. I need to keep up my angelic figure," Carter ran his hands over his overcoat.

"Aren't you burning up in that thing?"

"Not at all," Carter said.

"Where did you get it anyway; it seems dated?"

"An old friend gave it to me. Same with the hat. You should've seen what I wore before this." Carter gritted his teeth.

"Must be a good friend for you to still wear it after all this time."

"He's the best." Carter stepped onto the sand and sat on the brick wall that separated the Boardwalk from the beach. "Say, let's remove our shoes. Feel the sand between our toes."

"Sounds good to me," Stephanie said, following Carter's lead.

Both of them, shoes in hand, walked through the beach to the shoreline. Stephanie looked up and down the coast. "So,

Carter—Virginia or South Carolina? You commandeered all my personal belongings, or I'd flip for you for it. This is your trip, you call it."

Carter looked up the coast, then down the shoreline. He nodded and turned to their right.

"South it is." Stephanie followed, looking up at the sun nearing its midpoint. It was bright and clear; the steady sea breeze tossed her hair about. She thought about Jason, who would instinctively reach for his pocket and pull out a hair band. He always thought about her and was there when she forgot such things. A minor detail, something most people would overlook, but not Jason. It was the reason he was so good at his job. Details mattered. It was the things people couldn't see. It wasn't like writing where the final product was out in the open for all to see. With Jason's work, the details were behind walls and above ceilings. No one would know if you missed something—until it rained, or fifteen years later when things began to fall apart—when it really mattered. She had forgotten about those little things. The things that mattered.

"You coming?" Carter asked. He had gotten about ten yards from her before he turned and called to her.

"Yeah, I'm right behind you," Stephanie followed. She reached into the pocket of her sweatshirt where the type-writer ribbon was to ensure it had not unraveled, when another object grabbed her attention. She pulled it out—it was a hair tie. Black, just like the ones Jason kept in his pocket for her. She smiled, pulled her hair back out of her face, and put it up.

"You okay back there?"

"As if you didn't know," Stephanie said. She was catching on.

"Hey, Vanessa. It's Jason. Sorry to bother you at home on a Saturday, but have you heard from Stephanie? I tried to call her this morning, and her phone went straight to voicemail."

"No, I haven't," Vanessa said, but Jason could hear hesitance in her voice. "After wrapping up ahead of schedule, she let us go early. I know she was on a call with a client when I left for the day, though."

"Yes, she said someone dropped the ball and was ready to fire you guys. JMS is your big one, right?"

"Yeah?" Again, with hesitance.

"Stephanie said they are based in Wilmington and was heading down there to resolve the contract in person. You didn't know about this?"

"I was heading out of the office," Vanessa explained, "I didn't know it was *that* serious, or I'd never have left."

Jason could tell something wasn't right. "Okay."

"I will be honest, Jason, I turned my phone off today. In fact, the second I hit my car after leaving the office. I needed the break after this week. I'm sorry," Vanessa said. "I know she counts on me. And I should've checked my voicemail. I probably have a dozen messages from her because JMS *is* one of our long-term clients. We lose them, we may as well close up shop tomorrow. I don't blame her for heading down there."

With Vanessa's concern and vote of confidence, he felt reassured there was a reason for his wife's lack of communication.

"Thank you. Again, sorry to take you from your weekend. If you hear from her, ask her to call me."

"Will do, Jason," Vanessa said.

Jason wasn't sure what to do with the information. He

was concerned, and it wasn't like they hadn't gone extended periods without talking. He had his job; she had hers. But she had never taken an out-of-town trip alone before. This was a first. That's what had him most concerned.

The kids disrupted his silent musing by scrambling downstairs, both still in pajamas, their hair a mess, making him laugh. Evelyn, a brunette like her mother, had half a ponytail—or was it? "Look, dad," Joshua said. "I combed Evie's hair."

Fear gripped Jason, remembering the first time he attempted to comb his daughter's hair. He called Evelyn over, asking her to turn around. Sure enough, a wire bristle brush was half-tangled within her shoulder-length hair. His mind was going to be off his temporarily misplaced wife for a while as he needed to focus on dislodging this device from his daughter with as few tears as possible.

Jason released an exasperated sigh as he looked for an unbeginning endpoint. "How in the world?" he grumbled.

"Jujube," Joshua said.

"What?"

"Jujube," Joshua said again. "Mom put's jujube in Evie's hair to fix it."

"Somehow, son, I don't think candy will help your sister's predicament," Jason said as he lifted the brush handle.

"Ouch!" cried Evie.

"Sorry, sweetie," Joshua said, studying the brush, trying to figure out the puzzle.

"It's not candy, Daddy. That's silly. It's that gooey stuff in a green bottle in the cabinet."

"It's stinky," Evie said, with a crinkled nose. Her head shook, the comb waving back and forth. "Do something, Daddy."

"I'm trying, sweetie," Jason said. His hands danced around the brush, afraid to take hold of it again.

"Do you know where it is, Josh?"

"Yep. I'll go get it," he said and ran up the stairs.

Five minutes later, Joshua was back downstairs with the jujube—which Jason realized was jojoba oil.

Ten minutes later, and after a few more, *Ouch, Daddy's*, the comb was free, with the need for scissors.

"Okay," Dad said. "New rule. Nobody but Mom—and occasionally Dad—can comb Evie's hair. Is this understood?"

"Yes, Daddy," both kids said.

"Now, who's hungry for lunch?"

"Me!" came a duet of voices.

"Great. I am too. So, what are we going to eat?"

The kids wanted pancakes, the ones with the funny face, and there was only one place he knew of that served it that way, so he dressed the kids, drove, and hoped it was the one they spoke of. To his relief, the car filled with cheers when he pulled into the lot, and for the next hour, the kids battled on which part of the pancake face they would eat next.

Jason nursed a cup of coffee and nibbled on a BLT. He enjoyed watching the kids having fun with syrupy faces and fingers. He was glad they were young and oblivious to their parents' struggles. He prayed that he and Stephanie would get through this battle before they became old enough to understand. He prayed even harder that they wouldn't have to go through what he had witnessed so often among their friends and acquaintances—broken family.

Jason loved his wife and would do anything to keep her

and show his kids that love was worth fighting for. *When you care for someone, nothing should stand in the way.* The thought materialized in his mind as if from nowhere. He nodded his assent to the random thought. He knew that people were imperfect; that they—and he—needed a source of strength outside themselves. He just wasn't sure if he had it in him anymore, and he wasn't sure where to find it.

You need to talk to someone... someone who has been through this kind of struggle and came out victorious on the other side.

Once again a thought crossed his mind without any conscious effort on his part. Once again he nodded his agreement. He pulled out his phone and dialed. After two rings, a cheerful voice answered.

"Jason, honey. How are you?" Jason's mom asked.

"I'm doing good," Jason said.

"Hmm," his mom replied. "You don't sound convincing, dear."

Jason didn't respond to her clairvoyance. "The kids are asking about you. Can we come by after we finish our meal?"

"Sure, sweetie. We'd love to see them. While you're here, you can tell me why you're not answering my question."

Jason snickered. "See you soon, mom."

"We'll be here."

Chapter
Eleven

Saturday, November 22, 2025

"So, tell me about Texas, cowboy," Stephanie said as a wave crashed over their bare feet.

"I never said I was *from* Texas. It's just one of the places I've been through."

"But you have a connection to it."

"You could say that," Carter said.

Stephanie saw there was more than what he was saying. She had interviewed enough people to know when there was a story beneath the words.

"Okay, Carter, you know my story. What's yours?" Stephanie prodded.

"I'm on a mission, just like everyone else. I'm here doing what I love and accomplishing what the Lord put me here to do."

"And what's that? Besides sending people through time portals."

Carter laughed. "I'm here to help people connect with

what they are placed on earth to do. Most of the time, it works out well."

"And others?"

"Let's just say sometimes this task can become quite tasking," Carter said.

Stephanie nodded. There was certainly a story there—one worth reading for sure. "I understand. Some things are best left unsaid."

"Not necessarily. I simply leave details of my assignments where they belong, with each assignment. It would be impolite to share details of what you and I experience with whoever I encounter on my next assignment. It's only fair that I keep my previous affairs private for the same reasons. That is all."

"I get you," Stephanie nodded. It made sense. She certainly wouldn't want Carter to tell whomever he was to help next that he just came from an adulterous nag who turned down gelato.

"But to answer your question, yes, I loved being in Houston. I visited there twice, in fact. If you ever get the chance to go there, you must visit Davies Deli. It's a sandwich shop run by Mom and Pop Davies. Well, Mom passed a couple of years ago. But Pop and Aaron still run it."

"Aaron?"

Carter laughed. "Oh, my. That's a long story. Let's just say that he is the result of a prior successful mission. Anyhow, they run a sandwich shop in Houston that is most unique. They serve sandwiches like you wouldn't believe."

"I've eaten some interesting sandwiches," Stephanie said. With her reviews, she had eaten at many establishments, even experimental ones.

Carter laughed. "Not anything like *this*, I can assure you.

Try this," Carter stopped and leaned toward her as if telling a secret. "Meatloaf sub."

Stephanie's eyes narrowed, "Meatloaf sub? Don't you mean *meatball?*"

"Nope. Meat-*loaf.* Prepped as a loaf and sliced with the sauce and everything."

"What else?"

"Are you sure you're ready?"

"Go on," Stephanie said, folding her arms now.

"Spaghetti sub," Carter said, matching her pose.

"You have to be kidding me. Carter?"

"You wouldn't believe this establishment, Stephanie. Now, do you see why I love Houston? And this is beside their coffee houses and their *new* downtown library."

"New?"

"Well, it was new the last time I was there," Carter shrugged.

He and Stephanie continued their walk.

"So, Texas, huh?"

"Texas."

Stephanie thought about the city of Houston for a moment, then about the names he gave her. "So, this Aaron was like me?"

Carter became silent and took a few steps. She could tell it was a sensitive subject. He didn't want to talk about it. Stephanie wasn't sure if she could press or should just let it go. Another ten yards, and she knew it was not currently up for discussion, but then Carter did answer.

"Yes, in a way, he is," was all he said. Carter was silent for a bit, then he added, "You'll see."

A wave swept over their feet, nearly knocking both of them over. Carter grabbed her, steadying her.

"What does that—"

"Hey, look over there?" Carter interrupted and started to walk toward the land.

Stephanie followed, trying to keep pace. As they drew closer to the structure, she felt she recognized the place, although she had never been there. Then it occurred to her, she had written *about* the island. She snapped her fingers as they crossed the walkway and the condominium complex sign came into view. It was the business she was contracted with, Sand Dollar Condos. She recognized the signage in the shape of a giant sand dollar even before they reached it.

Stephanie stared at the sign and then at Carter, who knowingly nodded. One of the reasons she bid for this client was because sand dollars were special to her and Jason. With his encouragement, she contacted them, and with her convincing methods, landed two articles that triggered an uptick in clientele. That landed her a permanent retainer going on two years now.

The memory washed over her. Jason had taken her to Myrtle Beach for their one-month anniversary. While strolling together along the shoreline, he picked up a sand dollar, rinsed it in the surf, dried it with his shirt, then handed it to her. *How cheap is it to give a penny for your thoughts when you can offer a dollar,* he had said. Being new to love, it was the most romantic thing she had ever heard. Their sand dollar was unlike any other she had ever seen. It was odd-shaped and missing an eye, but she held it dear—until it wasn't. Neither of them was sure how their dollar got broken—maybe one of the kids. Not that it mattered. It was broken, and that was that.

"Sand Dollar Condos," Carter read the sign, shaking Stephanie from her reverie. "Doubt the price tag is as inexpensive."

"You would need more than a couple bucketfuls, I'm afraid, Carter," Stephanie said, looking up and shielding her eyes. "But it is a lovely place."

"You know it then?" Carter said.

Stephanie rolled her eyes. "You know very well that I do. I'm picking up on your game, mister. You have a plan for all you do. This walk was not just to *feel the sand between your toes.*"

"I'm just an innocent old man wanting to stroll along the Carolina shore," Carter said, placing his hat across his chest, "If we come across anything familiar, it is purely coincidental."

"Mmmhmm," Stephanie said. "So why are we here? You said there is a purpose in all things." She nodded toward the condos. "What's supposed to happen here?"

"Why don't you take a walk around and find out?"

As Stephanie stepped toward the complex, Carter said, "How long have you been writing for this client?"

Stephanie paused for a moment. "They are a long-term client. Year and a half, almost two. They are the ones that began my LLC."

"In those two years, have you ever been down to talk with them personally?"

"Once. At the beginning. Shelby and I met for lunch. Most of the work she and I do now is through emails and texts. But with corporate, they run three other hotels along the Carolina shore. This is just one of them."

"Do you write for all four?"

"No. The firm likes to have local writers handle the local area. So, they wanted writers close to those other hotels. I bid for them but was turned down. I tried the writer ploy of 'it's best to have all your contracts under one roof.' It didn't work. I understood the biz and let it be. No sense risking the old business in an attempt to get additional business, so I accepted the contract. And I have kept it, and they have agreed to every rate increase. Well, just two, but they knew a good deal when they saw it."

"So, there shouldn't be a reason for them to change their minds about using your services?"

"What are you getting at, Carter?"

"You had said a year and a half, almost two years. When is your contract up? You were the one who explained how personal service is the key to keeping clients happy and coming back to you. It is the reason Marshall Copywriting, LLC has been so successful. Yet, you have not visited your biggest client face-to-face since you signed the contract. Phone calls and Skyppie can only go so far."

Stephanie chuckled at his mispronunciation, but stopped when she thought about his question. It had been just before Thanksgiving when she had signed up with the *Sea Shell by the Seashore* company. She recalled rushing back to prepare for Thanksgiving with Jason's parents. The current contract would be up within a couple of weeks. She hadn't heard from them. But then, she had not contacted them either. She felt the urge to reach out to Vanessa to check on the status of that contract. But it was Saturday, and she had already given everyone the weekend off.

"You are standing in front of, or rather behind, the establishment, Stephanie," Carter said as if he had read her mind.

"What?"

"What is stopping you from walking into the office now? Would Shelby be here?"

"Most likely," Stephanie said, staring at the building.

"Could it make a difference to them? Especially if Shelby

passes on the word that their marketing lead stopped in to get a feel of the place for their next campaign?"

"You sound like a market manager, Carter. Who else have you helped over your career?"

Carter laughed. "You would be surprised how many ears have heeded the Lord's advice because He has chosen to make use of this old man."

Stephanie laughed, "You think I am in danger of losing this client? My longest client?"

"I cannot say. That might influence your actions. All I do is lead you to the place where you need to make a choice. I've probably overstepped my bounds, bringing you this far." Carter chuckled. "It's something Gabe gets on me about all the time."

"There you go, mentioning Gabe again. Who's Gabe? Is he your boss?"

Carter shrugged. "In a matter of speaking."

"I understand. You're just the writer."

"I'm sorry. I don't follow," Carter said.

"If God is the big boss, and I'm the assignment, this makes you the writer and Gabe the manager. You answer to the manager, and Gabe answers to the big boss; You and I are much alike, Carter Jennings," Stephanie said with a wink.

Carter's face contorted in thought, then he pursed his lips. "I supposed you could reason it in those terms. I wish I had thought of that when working with Aaron. He would've appreciated that allegory."

"Aaron?" Stephanie said.

"The deli and the sandwich," Carter reminded.

"Gotcha. Okay. Gabe; your boss. Aaron; sandwich genius. Carter Jennings; sent to save my soul. Got it."

Carter stuck out his thumb, "There you go. Now, are you going to check out this hotel, or will you let this opportunity shuck you by?"

"Ahhhhh," Stephanie said, pointing toward Carter, "Nice one. I see what you did there. Okay. Let's see what this Little Reminder holds. I'll be right back."

Stephanie crossed the bridge that led to the Sand Dollar Condos' property. The pool to her left had a family with kids laughing and playing. She looked up at the sky. The sun was tilting toward the opposite horizon. She figured it was late afternoon now. Carter still had never confirmed the day or time with her. Well, she could easily find out when she entered the office. There had to be a clock or a calendar on display somewhere. It wasn't Sunday—the office would be closed. Nor was it Friday—they hadn't arrived yet. Stephanie was pulled out of her contemplation by the girl screaming as her brother chased her around the pool, to which their parents admonished them about running on the wet deck.

She looked back at Carter, who swept-waved her on. She shrugged and turned the corner of the complex, following a sign that read Leasing Office.

The complex was easy enough to maneuver. There were signs guiding her to each place she would need to find. The pool she already had been to. The laundry facility was up and to the left, the gym was across the courtyard, and the game room was upstairs and behind her. She couldn't remember the facility having this many amenities. The thought if she lost this account it would be her own fault. She was definitely out of touch.

The directory also told her the main office was straight ahead inside the next building. After crossing the breezeway, she saw the smaller signs attached to the wall indicating the business office. When she reached for the handle, she suddenly felt under-dressed. She was about to meet a client, and she was in jeans, tennies, and a sweatshirt. Not to mention her hair in a windblown ponytail.

Stephanie stepped back, redid her tail, and fluffed out her slate grey top. She danced in place a couple of steps like Rocky Balboa and felt a bit more confident.

"Let's do this!" Stephanie said and reached for the handle.

Chapter
Twelve

Saturday, November 22, 2025

"It's already going on three, Mom," Jason said into his phone. "She said she would be home this afternoon."

"Well, Jason, it's still afternoon, sweetie," his mom said. "Maybe her phone died, or she lost it. There has to be an explanation. She wouldn't just not call you."

"I'm getting worried. It's ringing and going to voicemail, so the phone is on. So, it has a charge. That's a good thing. It's only been a day, and her phone holds a charge well on standby. I just don't know, Mom." Jason could tell he was getting upset.

"Jason, relax. I'm sure she's fine. Just pray about it and for her. She'll turn up."

Jason's mom always found a way to insert God into whatever situation they faced. *Pray about a headache, pray for a contract meeting, pray for the storm to rain on her tomato plants out back.* To her, there was a prayer for everything. *God is always listening, she would tell him.*

"I hope so," Jason said, rubbing the back of his neck. "So, how's Dad? What's he up to today?"

"Oh, you know your father. He's about to head to the flea market outside town, determined to find a keepsake. You know his collector's mind. That garage of his is full enough already. I don't know what you are going to do with all of his knickknacks and odds and ends when you clean up after us."

"Oh, Mom. I'm sure he will want to take them with him. He'll tell God he won't pass through the gates without them." Jason laughed.

"Perhaps, son." His mom laughed with him. "He always says when he picks up something that it would be something you would love. Remember when you two would hit those markets and swap meets when you were little?"

"Yes, I remember. Donuts and coffee, and cocoa for me. Then most of the morning hitting every meet in each town we could find."

"He'd be most proud of the little finds you'd picked up. He cherished those most."

"I never knew that," Jason said.

"It's true, Jason. I can assure you, what you see on the shelves is just a fraction of what your pop has hidden away," his mom said. "Now, don't you go telling him any of this. He would just go denying it."

"I won't. But it matters," Jason said, then after a pause, "And you're right."

"About what?"

"Stephanie. I'm probably worried about nothing. Even her coworker reminded me that we've gone hours without contact before. Why should this be any different? It's just—this time it *feels* different."

"As I said, sweetie. Put it in God's hands, and all will be fine," she said.

"I will. Okay, we're about ready to head that way. Is it okay to drop the kids with you? I think I want to find an old man digging through a pile of junk."

"Go ahead and let my precious angels stay with their grandma. I'd love to spend the afternoon with them. And it would excite your pop to see your face in the crowd. Hurry up. He's just getting in the truck. I won't tell him your plan."

"Yes, ma'am. I'm on my way." Jason disconnected and bundled the kids into the car where they daydreamed of homemade cookies and cold milk.

Jason saw his Pop's pick-up in the lot and parked next to it. He was surprised the flea market was still packed—it was nearing 3:30. He remembered these markets used to become ghost towns by 2:00. That they were still going strong would certainly make his dad happy. Jason made his way to the entrance and waded through the crowd, looking for his father's unmistakable signature—a bright blue N.C. Tar Heel's hat.

After a couple of aisles with no luck, he wondered if he was in the right place. He stopped to look around. *Maybe Pop hit a food truck first before coming,* he mused. It was in the seventies, but his dad drank coffee any time of the day, and midday snacking was his thing.

Jason returned to the midway, found the food court, and noticed the improvements. All types of vendors, from tacos to brisket, sausage wraps, and desserts. *Lots of changes since the last time I was here,* he thought. But still no blue cap. He searched again, looking for a familiar face, just in case his father wasn't wearing his signature cap today. Nothing out of the ordinary; regular ball caps, beanies, and a man in a tweed cap, but no one resembling his father.

Jason made one more visual pass over the food court and stopped with a huff.

"You just missed him," a voice spoke.

Jason looked down at a man sitting at a table, eating what looked like ice cream. He was wearing the tweed cap.

"Just missed who?"

"Your father, Jason. He ordered a coffee and a couple of tacos. When he finished those, he headed off," Carter nodded toward the crowd.

"You're a friend of my father?"

"Not exactly," Carter said, taking a spoonful of his snack.

"Who are you then?"

"My name is Carter Jennings."

Jason looked Carter over, then it occurred to him, "Wait a second. Tweed hat. You're the guy who found my menu, aren't you?"

Carter nodded. "Guilty as charged. Well, not *guilty* in the sense of what you may think it would mean."

"Meaning you didn't steal it," Jason said.

"Correct."

"Then how did you get it?"

"Let's just say it was given to me," Carter said, pointing to the chair across from him. "Please have a seat."

"I need to catch up with my dad."

"There is time for that. Please. Sit."

Jason looked over his shoulder, then back at Carter. Carter motioned to the chair again, and Jason sat. He did want to find his dad, but this was the man who found his missing menu—this was worth a little bit of time to explore.

"You have my attention, Carter. Explain."

"As I told your wife, I found it in a box, and I was told to give it back to you. That's all."

"Someone *told* you to give it to us?"

"Something like that. And now it is back in your hands, and you have the blessing of it once again."

"And you can't reveal who told you."

"I would prefer not to. My source gets kinda jumpy when I break protocol."

"Your source? You sound like my wife. She is always talking about sources."

"So we are on the same page, then," Carter said.

"I suppose. I'm just glad to have it back. Nothing else of value was taken that wasn't covered by the insurance. I guess a thank you is in order." Jason extended a hand.

Carter accepted it with a tooth-filled grin. "You are welcome."

"So, what can I do for you, Carter?"

"I think it's more about what I can do for you?"

"You can help me? You don't even know me."

"Well, God's the one who can help you. I'm just the one He works through."

"*God* sent you?" Jason said, his eyebrows raised.

"Yes, He did. He knows the weight you are carrying right now. I could feel it just watching you walk up here. I can feel it upon your shoulders now as you're sitting across from me."

"And what is that?"

"Stephanie."

Jason wasn't sure what to think about what this stranger was saying. How could he know that he was concerned about his wife?

"I'm not sure what you are getting at," Jason said, hiding behind the fact that this man was a stranger.

"Oh, I'm sure you do. And it's okay. You don't know me from Adam. And I don't blame you for not wanting to divulge your personal life to a stranger. But I can assure you, I have the best of intentions."

"Regardless. While I appreciate you returning our lost menu, I don't see how that would make me want to open the door to my personal life."

"Even if it would comfort you about her recent lack of communication?"

"Okay. How do you know about that?" Jason said.

"I can assure you, all is well. She is safe and not in any harm."

"Then you need to explain quickly, Carter."

"Right now, your wife is with a client, trying to keep her business afloat."

"So that wasn't a lie, then?"

"I can assure you Stephanie is in a business meeting as we speak."

Jason felt relief. He had nearly convinced himself she had headed to the coast for a tryst with a secret client, which was the reason for the radio silence.

"Then why isn't she answering my calls?"

Carter shrugged. "All I can tell you is that she's meeting with her clients now."

"How do you know all of this, Carter?"

"Let's just say we have common interests," Carter said.

"Are you always this vague?"

"I try not to be. I feel I'm being quite transparent with the information I am able to give."

"I just wish she would reach out and let me know she was okay."

"Give her time. She may need to get into a position where it's okay to talk."

Jason wasn't so sure that would be anytime soon. Even if she was in a meeting, there was no guarantee she would call him afterward. They had no arrangements to do so, even when they were local.

"I need to find her. Maybe I should drive down there. She might need my support."

"Now, don't go making any rash decisions. Remember why you are here?"

Jason had almost forgotten. "Dad."

"Yes. He needs you as well. Finding you here will make his day."

As if on cue, a voice that sounded like an older version of Jason called, "Son?"

Jason looked up, and walking toward them was his pop—in a blue Tar Heels cap.

"Dad," Jason said, standing and accepting his embrace.

"What are you doing here? And who's your friend?"

"I came here looking for you. Mom said you'd be here. This is Carter. He's a friend. I was walking by, and he spotted me. I must've gotten lost in conversation, sorry. Carter Jennings, Eldon Marshall."

Jason's dad extended his hand; Carter stood and accepted it, "Pleased to meet you, Carter. You visit here often? I don't believe I recognize you."

"No, sir. This is my first visit to this market," Carter said.

"Lovely place. I must make it back here again. Excellent gelato. Well, Jason. It was a pleasure seeing you. I will let you get on with your father and son activities. I must be on my way. I am expected somewhere, and I'm running late."

"Thank you for your insight, Carter. I will consider all you've said," Jason said.

"It would be appreciated. Have a blessed day," Carter said, tipped his hat, and walked away.

"So how do you know him, Jason?" his dad asked.

"He finds things. Kinda like you do, dad. I think the two of you would get along."

Jason and his father spent the afternoon reconnecting, just like old times. Only now he wasn't a child picking up useless trinkets that would find their way into a storage box in his pop's garage. These were moments that reminded both of them why they do what they do. Jason realized he needed to slow down, that his life was just too busy. It took recognizing the pace his father walked through the market. He figured that his dad must've looked at something at every vendor. Some of them he knew by name. It showed him that some things don't change.

"Do you visit every booth, Dad?"

"Not every one, son. Just the ones that speak to me."

"They speak to you?"

"Each booth has its own vibe. Some of them will tell you if there is anything worth purchasing."

"Have you always had this sense when swap meet swapping?"

"Not always. I used to come with a purpose. Then I used to come out of habit. And for a while, just to get away. Now, it is my exercise and a way to meet with friends."

"The vendors?" Jason asked.

"Many of them, yes. But others are wanderers like me. Sometimes we will meet in the food court area. Just not today. It's too late for that. We usually meet early in the morning. But for some reason, I felt I needed to be here this afternoon. And who do I see? You! So now I know why I came this late."

"I spoke to Mom, and she told me you'd be here; that's why I'm here," Jason said.

"Hmm," Jason's dad said. "Well, I'm glad you did. I'm enjoying our time together."

"I am as well," Jason said.

They continued their walk, talking with vendors about the nice weather—Thanksgiving in a couple of weeks and plans with family. Jason's dad talked about having him along and about how proud he was of him as a home builder. He even handed out cards to those who said they had children looking to buy a home. It made Jason smile to see his dad glow when he spoke of him. He wondered if it was this way when he wasn't present. He had to laugh. During a more extended discussion, he began to window shop. The vendor had so many items to look through that one could get lost in their small space. He supposed they must've had someone remove or clean out a storage unit because they were so full, from clothing to kitchen gadgets to electronics.

They had a table designated to books; *Stephanie would appreciate this,* Jason thought. Famous trilogies and magical adventures; he knew she liked to read mystery thrillers. Then among the piles he saw a book that seemed out of place. It looked like a scoop of ice cream in the middle of darkness. The Neapolitan cover struck him, so he picked it up.

Jason gasped. In the looked in the lower right corner he saw the initials S.A.C.

Chapter
Thirteen

Saturday, November 22, 2025

A single tone announced Stephanie's entrance to the office. The room was laid out like a typical family living space. She expected as much. Let the prospective tenant get the feel of walking into their home as they arrive. Nodding her approval, she closed the door behind her and walked through the room. Of course, everything was top-of-the-line; no Walmart specials here. Hardwood floors, high-end leather couches; the glass coffee and end tables exuded style, and it wasn't just the aromatherapy plugin.

Brochures about the property and their amenities laid on the pass-through between the dining area to the kitchen. She knew about most of them having written about them. Picking one up she learned they offered more floor-plans than the size of the property revealed, from studio apartments up to three-bedroom condos. She looked at the wall for a map, as some properties had, but didn't see one. Perhaps the owner didn't want to take away from the home ambiance by making it look like a business. It was most likely in the office that she'd soon see.

"Good afternoon," a male voice called from halfway down the hall. It reminded her she had yet to search for a clock.

Stephanie peeked through the pass-through into the kitchen; the clock on the stove said it was just after 2:30.

"Good afternoon," Stephanie echoed as a slender older gentleman in a suit appeared. Odd for an apartment manager to be wearing a coat and tie, much less on a Saturday.

"I'm Gerald McManus, Property Manager," the dark-haired man said, "how can I be of assistance? Are you looking to rent or perhaps lease one of our fabulous residences?"

Stephanie had to refocus before she spoke. Gerald McManus? *The* Gerald McManus? As in *McManus* Weedon Enterprises, who owned the properties she was writing for? This was impossible. Or was it? Stephanie felt the ribbon burning a hole at her stomach.

She must've been silent too long because Mr. McManus tilted his head. "Are you okay, miss?"

Stephanie smiled with a slight chuckle. "Yes, Mr. McManus. Sorry. I'm fine. I was just caught off-guard. I wasn't expecting to see *you* here."

Mr. McManus squinted at her. "Do we know each other?"

"Only by proxy, sir," Stephanie said. "My name is Stephanie Marshall. It's been my honor to make your place shine on video and in print for the past two years. I've been working with Shelby, but I haven't seen her for a while. I was down here this weekend with a friend and wanted to stop in to say hello."

"A while, you say?" Mr. McManus folded his arms and leaned back. "Try since you signed the contract two years ago and told her you wouldn't leave her behind."

"I'm sorry?" Stephanie said.

"She explained that other than a few phone calls asking for more money from us, she only saw you face-to-face at that initial meeting. Is this accurate, Ms. Marshall?"

Stephanie wasn't sure how to respond. His words were accurate, but she and Shelby spoke regularly. It wasn't like she was hanging the complex out to dry. In fact, she poured more into this campaign than most other adverts she wrote. She considered Shelby part of the Marshall Copywriting family. This was the first time she had heard of their dissatisfaction. Why now?

"Mr. McManus, it is true that I don't make it down here in person as often as I would like, but I keep in touch over the phone as needed. I thought we had a good relationship. I was unaware of Shelby's or your unhappiness with my performance."

"Well, now you do. And I suppose it's good you are here today, Ms. Marshall."

"It is?"

"Yes, a postage stamp is saved by not having to mail your official notice. We will not be renewing our contract with you."

Stephanie felt the gut punch. She had never been fired before. She'd experienced not being picked up after a trial piece but never terminated.

"I'd like to speak to Shelby, please," Stephanie said.

"Ms. Marshall, I don't know what good it would do. *We* are the client. She works for us. She passes information on to us, and we make the decisions. I'm sorry things couldn't continue. But as they say, all good things must come to an end."

"I can understand that. I want to talk to Shelby, please."

"Your contract is still active until the end of the month.

You are still employed, so have at it." Mr. McManus nodded Stephanie toward the hallway.

Knowing the floor plan, she passed the first bedroom and the hall bath; the back bedroom was where she felt she needed to go. A couple of mumbled voices grew louder. Stephanie tapped on the partially closed door.

"Shelby? Shelby, may I come in?"

"I know that voice," said the other familiar voice. "Come on in."

Stephanie entered the room. With Shelby sat another woman, about the same age as the man in the living room. She was also dressed in business attire. Shelby was dressed down. Stephanie assumed she was in on her day off, perhaps called in to handle some business emergency. A sour thought made her grimace. Perhaps *she* was the business emergency.

"May I help you, miss?" the woman across from Shelby asked.

"I'm your writer, ma'am. The one you currently employ, and the one you are going to keep. I'm here to assure you I have no intention of accepting the 'we no longer need your services' letter without a fight," Stephanie answered, then turned to Shelby. "Shelby. I'd like to speak with you privately, if that's alright."

Shelby looked at her visitor, then back to Stephanie. She nodded. "Ms. Gentry, will you excuse us, please."

Ms. Gentry, more politely than Mr. McManus, nodded in acceptance, then stood. She stopped at the door, "You're Stephanie Marshall?"

Stephanie wasn't sure how to reply, but honesty always seemed best. "Yes, ma'am."

Ms. Gentry smiled. "Excellent work, Ms. Marshall." She turned and exited the room.

Stephanie watched the door shut and then turned her attention to Shelby. She gestured toward the door where the older woman exited. "What was that about?"

"She's on your side," Shelby said. "But we'll get to that. I can't believe they called you down here only to fire you."

Stephanie wasn't sure where to begin. Again she turned to honesty as the best policy. "They didn't call me down here. It's just a coincidence. I came down with a friend, and since I was in the neighborhood and I haven't been this way since we signed our contract I felt I should stop by and say hello. And I have to say, Shelby, *wow*, this place is more amazing in person. I am kicking myself that I haven't moved down here yet."

Shelby laughed. "It's not too late. We have a couple of vacancies. But you would either need to get a divorce for the efficiency or have a kid or two because the only other available option is a three-bedroom."

Stephanie managed a slight laugh. "The two kids we already have. I'll have to see how Jason feels about living on the ocean. But I can't guarantee anything." Stephanie half wondered what it would be like to have the Atlantic Ocean as your backyard.

Shelby looked to the door and shook her head. "Girl, I just don't get it. You saw all the add-ons out there. You know we are at near capacity. We have *your* advertising to thank for that.

"The complex up the road is at seventy-five percent. The one to our south, The Palms, is at eighty percent. They both need work, and they try to comp with us. The Palms has greater beach access but we can charge more because of the facility and the rooms; access is secondary." Shelby lowered her voice, then pointed to the door. "But *he* doesn't see that."

Shelby sat back, folded her arms, and shook her head. "I'm fighting for you, Stephanie, but with that man everything is about the bottom line. He thinks you're overcharging him. He doesn't understand marketing has been in the budget for years, even before you, and he has always signed off on it."

"I'm not cheap," Stephanie admitted, eyebrow raised.

"But you're not overpriced," Shelby responded. "You would be surprised how much some agencies charge to advertise for a place like this." Shelby waved her hand around. "You're a bargain compared to some agencies."

"I assume you've shopped other agencies?" Stephanie said.

Shelby nodded. "It's my job to get the most bang for the boss's buck. After your first increase, I looked. Every other agency wanted more. I even shopped those online sites where you can pay by the job."

"Shelby, you did not," Stephanie said. "Most are amateurs, and it's a crap shoot. You may find a diamond in the rough, but most of the time you get what you pay for. Trust me. I'm an agency. I have writers under me, and I have tried to hire writers through them. Yeah, I shot myself in the foot more than once and had to rewrite pieces. I hire word-of-mouth now."

"Yes, So I've learned."

"Learned?!" Stephanie said. "Wow. I had no idea."

"That's the point. You weren't supposed to. And you are still employed, and you got your rate increase because you are worth every cent. And it was right about the time of that first increase that we began to see the turnaround here. As you grew, your quality grew. As that happened, our business flourished. More people knocked on the door and said it was because they read about us on this site or heard about it from so and so. This place is a success because it's a great facility, but also because of the work you put into it." Shelby pointed to the door, "They just don't see it."

Once again, Stephanie was speechless by the testimony of the impact of her accomplishment. Her words had changed someone's life. They impacted Shelby, and they drew many individuals and families to this place where they could create a home.

Her mantra to her staff of writers had always been, *Words Matter!* But if she was honest with herself, recently that mantra had grown stale. It was just... words. Now, seeing Shelby's face light up when she talked about how her job had changed because of what Stephanie was doing—she had a fresh realization... *Words Mattered.*

Shelby wiped a tear, breathed, and looked to the door, "Hey, Mr. Man! Get in here!"

The door opened, and first, Ms. Gentry appeared. Her wide-eyed expression revealed that the informal address was unacceptable. Mr. McManus followed, appearing more than a trifle annoyed.

"Can I help you?" Mr. McManus said, a slight edge to his voice.

"I have chosen to retain Ms. Marshall as our staff writer."

"I'm sorry, but that decision is not yours to make. It is mine, and I've already made it. We no longer require her services."

"Mr. McManus, if you choose to cut ties with Ms. Marshall, then you choose to end your relationship with me as well. Your end date for her services will be my end date of employment."

Mr. McManus' expression changed from uptight to concern, "But you can't do that. Who will manage the Sea Shell?"

"Not my problem," Shelby shrugged.

Mr. McManus pursed his lips. "Fine. You both can be replaced. It will actually save me money. I can hire two part-time managers at half the pay. Then I won't have to concern myself with benefits. It'll save me tons of money." Mr. McManus grinned. "Thank you, Shelby, you're actually doing me a favor. And, Ms. Marshall, marketers are a dime a dozen nowadays. I can find someone like you for pennies on the dollar."

Shelby stood, "We'll see when tenants' contracts are up, and you need to either retain those tenants or bring in new ones. Then we'll see who's saving money and who's asking who for favors, Mr. McManus. Now, if there won't be anything else, I'd like to get back to the rest of my day. Wouldn't want to have to bill you for an after-hours service call."

Chapter
Fourteen

Saturday, November 22, 2025

Stephanie and Shelby discussed the final marketing projects that were already in the works. There were two articles in the queue, and Lauren had written a few additional travel advertisements for the city that tied in the complex. It was one of those *visitors-become-tenants* campaigns. The complex had two vacancies and filling them quickly was a priority.

"With their sizes, I don't think they should be a problem. Especially the studio," Shelby said. "With college students graduating soon and seeing the ads, it may get mom and dad to open the pocketbook. Lauren did a perfect job. And I love what you've set up."

"I know. Lauren has never let me down. I can't wait to get back and finalize this with her," Stephanie said. "I'm just sad this will be our final collaboration. But I don't think you should quit on my account. There are always other writers."

"McManus just doesn't realize the reason for this place's success is you. It has nothing to do with what I've done.

He's the fool. I'm nervous about what will happen when you're gone."

"Nonsense," Stephanie said. "You can just take what I've been doing and rehash it. I give you full permission to do that."

"That's just it. I don't *want* to do that. He needs to recognize your worth and not toss you to the curb. He should at least apologize for how he treated you. I meant everything I said. I don't want to continue without you."

Stephanie appreciated her vote of confidence, and while she didn't want to discourage her, she was more concerned that Shelby's impulse action could leave her with an unemployment hangover.

"I just ask you to think about it. I'm honored you feel this way about our relationship. But please think about your family before you do anything you can't take back. You and your boy need this."

Shelby smiled and agreed to sleep on it. They decided to talk before the holiday, just to see if the two rooms had been filled and if the campaign had been successful. That would most likely be their final meeting.

Stephanie looked at the clock. It was later than she expected. *Carter must've sent in the calvary by now. Or maybe he just wandered off in search of another gelato,* she thought wryly. She left the office, choosing to head left instead of the way she came in. She wanted to see the front of the complex. She remembered a waterfall in the photos and wanted to see it firsthand. Distinctiveness was one thing that intrigued her about writing, discovering something about a location that pulled her in; for her, this water feature was it.

Stephanie walked around another building, still amazed by how much larger the complex was than it appeared from the beach. When she reached the street, she noticed how far from the highway it was, pleased that the business was so successful. It was by far the most attractive in the stretch of complexes in the area. It almost felt out of place. She was proud of what Shelby had accomplished. *How could they just let her go?*

As she rounded the entrance, she could hear and smell the water flow. Then she saw the rock waterfall. It was made from beautiful cream-colored stone. The water flowed for about ten yards along a pebble-laden shore into a shallow pool with palm trees on each side. The far end of the stream had larger rocks and boulders where people could sit and enjoy the peaceful solitude. Stephanie followed the stream and sat on one of the stones.

She leaned over and ran her fingers through the flowing water, recounting the last several hours. *What do I do now?* she pondered. *I'm about to lose our biggest account. I nearly had an affair with an employee. I still have to go home and face the music about that. And I'm walking around with an angel telling me I need to find my way back to God.*

Stephanie wasn't sure what to do about any of it, but the ambiance of the place helped to ease her mind. As the water rippled over the stones, something caught her eye. While most of the stones were darker grey or brown, this one was a bright white. It glimmered through the current, and Stephanie leaned over to pick it up. It wasn't a rock. It was a seashell—a sand dollar. It didn't seem out of place, given the location's name, but there was nothing else like it in the stream or pool. In fact, she could see no other shells of any kind within the pool. As Stephanie dried the shell, she almost dropped it. It was missing an eye.

Carter stood staring out into the ocean. Another wave crashed, and the foam tickled his bare feet. He thought it all felt the same: West coast, east coast, southern gulf.

"Is this what I think it is?" Stephanie asked as she made her way to him.

"What do you think it is?"

"It looks like the shell Jason gave me on our walk along Myrtle Beach. But that's not possible. That shell is in Evansville, *and* it's broken. Carter, this is identical, the scarring, even down to the missing eye," Stephanie said, caressing the shell, eyeing it up against the sunlight.

Carter smiled. "It's a beautiful shell."

Stephanie matched his grin. "That it is."

He watched as she admired the shell, looked to the sea, then back to him.

"What's on your mind?" Carter said.

"Wondering how you did it?"

Carter scrunched his eyebrows. "Did what?"

"You know exactly what I'm talking about. This shell was broken. Now it's mended. I can reason how you got it here. You would've had to bring it with you. But this *is* the same shell. I have no doubt. I've stared at it too many times to be tricked by an impostor."

Carter nodded. "It was in my box." He had no intention of elaborating. The gift of ambiguity was a game he had mastered. It was one he enjoyed engaging in with his assignments. Stephanie opened the door to this fun—he chose to run with it.

"One day, you will have to show me this box. I'm sure it has many interesting items."

Carter chuckled. Maybe he was giving away too much. The only other person who knew about his box was Aaron. It was his inquisitive mind that drew him to it and to own it for a moment in time. Carter should know by now that throwing a bone at a writer would only stir the kettle and get the imagination going.

"That it does, that it does," Carter said.

"I suppose you are going to tell me that God miraculously mended my broken shell?" Stephanie asked as another wave washed over their feet.

"You don't believe that God can mend something that is broken?" Carter asked, giving her his full attention.

"When talking about something inanimate, like a shell, it takes more than a spoken word to mend."

"Since you brought it up, what about the animate?"

Stephanie exhaled and looked at the shell. Carter hoped her thoughts were taking her back to her husband and their walk, as was the intention of this particular Little Reminder. His being on the beach after her finding it was also a trigger.

Another wave crashed. It drenched their feet as a tear drenched her cheek. "Do I really need to answer that?"

"I love a good story," Carter reminded.

Stephanie laughed. "God doesn't make you privy to my entire life story? I thought you knew everything."

"I'm not omniscient, Stephanie. Only God knows everything. I may be an angel of the Lord, but I'm not that type of angel. I only know what I learn about you and from what you tell me."

"So, what do you know?"

"I know the shell is as special to you and Jason as was the

menu; it is what brought you two together. It reminds you that you love him and that your relationship is important."

"Yeah, but it is more than that, Carter. I realized something finding that shell."

"And what is that?"

"The little things. It's all those little reminders I forgot about Jason."

"Tell me more," Carter said, then he pointed down shore. "Let's walk while we talk, shall we?"

Stephanie clenched the shell and followed. "It goes beyond the menu and the shell. Jason and I have those moments where we would simply get caught up in each other. A heart drawn on the steamed-up mirror, a just-because love note on a sticky pad, or a spur-of-the-moment phone call. I never realized how much those tiny things meant to me. We do them out of habit, but those small things matter. It's the glue that make us work." Stephanie paused. "Or made us work. I've neglected them lately. Now I've gone and done this. I bet he thinks I don't love him anymore. I wonder if he still loves me?"

"But it's still something the two of you can work on. It's never too late," Carter said, nodding toward the dry sand. He led, she followed.

"After what I've done? I don't know," Stephanie said. "I wouldn't be surprised if he was already looking for someone else." Stephanie shook her head. "No, that's not Jason. He is faithful to the core. I'm the rotten one. Look at me."

"It's never too late to change. Think about it. You didn't cheat. You didn't sin, Stephanie."

"*You* changed that. You gave me something that put me to sleep and woke me up in another world," Stephanie said.

"I did no such thing," Carter said. "All I did was talk to

you. I don't know what happened after that—other than I found you the next day in the coffee shop."

"You mean ten years in the past," Stephanie laughed.

"Well yeah, there is that," Carter echoed her sentiment.

"So, what do we do now?"

"Let's head back to the hotel," Carter directed, "I think your car may be waiting for you."

"I gotta go, Dad," Jason said once he found him in the small crowd.

"Why, what's wrong?"

Jason held up the book. "This is Stephanie's Bible."

"Yeah, so?" his dad said. Then realization set in. "Oh, wow. And you found it here? Where?"

"At the next vendor," he pointed to the stack of darkened books.

"Yeah, that would've stood out." His dad looked at the Neapolitan mystery. "Are you positive?"

"Beyond a shadow of a doubt." Jason handed him the Bible. "Look at the bottom corner."

His father pulled out his glasses and focused where his son had pointed. "S.A.C. Well, you have me there. Those are her initials. And you are sure this is hers?"

"Whose else could they be? I need to find her. This can't be a coincidence."

"What makes you say that, son? Does this have anything to do with your friend I saw you with earlier?"

"Yes, but I don't have time to explain, Dad. Trust me, everything is okay. I just need to find Stephanie. Can I leave the kids with you and Mom till I get back?"

"I trust you, Jason. You do what you need to do. Just tell me about it later."

"That I will do. It's an interesting story," Jason said as he left.

Chapter
Fifteen

Saturday, November 23, 2030

"Missus? Missus?"

Stephanie was awakened by someone tapping her shoulder. She snapped up to see a confused cleaning lady with a bottle of Windex in her hand. "Missus? What are you doing in this room?"

Stephanie shook the heavy feeling from her head. "What's going on? How did I get here? Where's Carter?"

"I don't know who Carter is. Miss, why are you in this room?"

Stephanie looked around. It looked like the room she had slept in the night before, yet somehow different. She rubbed her temple; the hungover feeling had returned.

What is happening to me?

The cleaning lady was still speaking, and very loudly. Stephanie fan-waved her away. "Can you please not talk so loud? I'm trying to think," Stephanie said. She tried to stand, but the room began to spin, and she fell back into the bed.

The maid didn't seem to notice or care. "Ma'am, why are you in this room?"

"This is *my* room," Stephanie answered, her arm covering her eyes. "I checked in last night."

"This room is supposed to be vacant. What is your name?"

"Stephanie Marshall," she said, slowly sitting up. "What time is it?"

"Almost ten," the maid said. "Ms. Marshall, you need to leave this room immediately."

"This is my room. I paid for it last night." Stephanie said, rubbing the back of her neck. "My check out isn't until two. Call downstairs and confirm."

The maid went to the phone, but it wasn't on the nightstand; it was now on a desk on the other side of the room. The desk that was no longer white, nor was it brown. It was made of glass and carried a business tone, much like the rest of the room.

Memories and the out of sync timeline started to creep back into her consciousness again. Kenneth, his advances, her acceptance; their trip from Evansville.

What happened with Kenneth?

She started to panic, then remembered.

Nothing.

She came to the room and passed out. Then woke up here. At least she *thought* she came to her room. But that felt like ages ago. Stephanie's temples ached as she continued trying to piece together what was happening.

The maid hung up the phone. "The front desk doesn't have any record of this room being occupied, Ms. Marshall."

"That's not possible. I came here with a man; his name is Kenneth Alistair. You need to check his name."

"Look, ma'am, I'm just part of the cleaning staff. The front desk can check that information for you, but you need to please leave so I can prepare this room for our next guest."

Stephanie didn't want to press any further. She knew she wasn't getting anywhere. She nodded and stumbled to the bathroom to pack, but she couldn't find her suitcase. She checked the closet, the fiberglass dresser that had been wooden before, and even under the bed, which drew a huff from the cleaning lady, but she didn't find anything.

"You didn't happen to see a suitcase when you came in here?" Stephanie asked.

"The only thing I found when I came in here was you," the disgruntled maid replied with a scowl.

"Thank you. I'm leaving now," Stephanie said.

As the elevator descended, Stephanie prepared for the worst. If the room was different, the lobby would be night and day. Her mind was swimming with memories that she wasn't sure were hers. There was a walk on a beach, an office confrontation, and a talk in a coffee shop about the future—her future. She attempted to shake the cobwebs from her brain as the bell sounded for the lobby floor. The door opened, and as she expected, the lobby was completely unfamiliar.

The front desk was still to her left, the restaurant with the coffee bar was just ahead, and the waiting area was to her right; but all of their features had been altered. Stephanie spoke to the front desk clerk, but he was as helpful as the cleaning lady had been. There was no record of her checking in—or out. Nor did he have any idea who Kenneth Alistair was.

The general manager approached, apparently alerted to the situation by the maid.

"Ma'am, we need to know how you intend to pay for the room you obviously slept in?" the manager said.

"I don't know," Stephanie answered. I have no idea what happened to my purse or my luggage. All I had when I woke up this morning is what I'm wearing. But my name is Stephanie Marshall, and I live in Evansville. I own Marshall Copywriting Services, so I'm good for the money. You can call my husband, Jason." Stephanie gave him the number, and the manager dialed.

"Hello, Mr. Marshall. Yes, this is Robert Evans. I am the manager at Hotel by the Sea. I have Stephanie Marshall here. She is without identification and claims to be your spouse. Can you verify her?" Robert was silent for a moment, then looked her up and down. "Five-eight, dark brown hair below shoulder length, perhaps one seventy-five—

"Hey!" Stephanie retorted, "I'm no more than one-sixty soaking wet."

Evans ignored her and continued with his description. "Green eyes that are glaring at me because I have apparently miscalculated her weight."

More silence.

"Mmmhmm. Yes, I will convey the message, sir." Evans hung up the phone.

"Well, what did he say?" Stephanie said.

"I'm not sure you want to hear the message, ma'am," Robert said.

Stephanie's face contorted. "I don't follow? What did my husband say?"

"You mean *ex*-husband, ma'am," the manager replied. "Not to put too fine a point on it, he said that *you* divorced *him* five years ago, and that if you need help you should call your lover."

Stephanie felt dizzy, and the room went dim. "I need to sit down. I'm going to vomit."

"Not in here, you're not," Evans warned. Then pointed to the lobby, "There is a restroom—"

"Yeah, I know where the restroom is," Stephanie snapped, then took a deep breath and more calmly replied, "I'm sorry, thank you."

"Your bill?"

"Give me a moment. I'll be right back," Stephanie walked to the restroom and made friends with the porcelain.

After washing up, she eyed herself in the mirror and saw a woman who looked like she deserved what she had gotten.

But what happened? she wondered. *I divorced Jason—five years ago? How is that possible? I only left town last night. I haven't even had time to eat breakfast at the diner. The diner!*

Stephanie slapped the restroom door open and headed for the diner. Thankfully it was still there, with its new-age counter setting. But the older man in a tweed cap was not sitting at the end of the counter where he was supposed to be. A couple with helmets by their side was sitting in his place.

Did I imagine him? Am I going crazy?

After a glance around the restaurant, Stephanie found a booth and sat; perhaps that would help jog her memory. *Some people say taste and scents have tremendous effect on memory. Maybe a meal will trigger some of mine that seem to be missing.*

She ordered a plate of eggs, French toast, and a small stack of pancakes. She finished the last of her coffee, and though her stomach was full, her mind was as empty. *What do I do now? I still have to settle up with the manager for last night's bill, and now for the meal.*

Stephanie looked toward the exit. For the first time in

her life, she considered skipping out on a bill. It wouldn't be difficult. When the waitstaff wasn't watching, she would head to the restroom, which was close to the entrance, then walk out as if she had paid the bill. No one would question her; they would assume she had paid. It sounded like a plan.

Unfortunately, the dining room kept steadily busy, and it stayed that way for the better part of an hour. Stephanie asked for a newspaper and read as she nursed a few refills. That's when she learned the year was 2030—five years after the time period she would consider home. The news on the TV screen informed her that mid-term elections had just taken place and that, as usual, one party was not happy and was accusing the other party of gross election interference.

Some things never change, Stephanie thought. She sipped her cup and considered her next move. She figured either this was a cruel joke, she was sick and needed help, or something bigger was in play. She could remember bits and pieces of the older man in the tweed cap. Seeing the restaurant bought back more memories. He *had* been sitting at *that* counter; only *that* counter was brown and older, well, older to her. She shook her head to dislodge the conflicting images; it was too much.

Stephanie took a feigned sip from her now empty cup. Right now, the only waitress on the floor was taking an order from a couple in a corner booth. The waitress left them and pushed through the swinging doors to the kitchen at the far end of the diner. It's *now or never*, Stephanie thought. She picked up her only belonging and headed for the entrance. As she passed the register, a voice called to her, making her head spin.

"Skipping out on two bills in one day? Not very prudent, Stephanie," the familiar voice called.

His tone was like a key that opened a door, and Stephanie remembered everything. *Carter.* The second before she woke up in that crummy bed, she had been walking along the shore of a sandy beach with the owner of that voice. They were on their way to her car when she became dizzy. He caught her when she fell. *Had he prepared for it?* She remembered a soft landing.

"Carter Jennings," Stephanie began walking toward him, "What in the world is going on here? Where, rather, when are we? The paper…" Stephanie looked around, then leaned closer and sat on the stool next to him. "The paper says it's 2030. How is that possible when it's 2025?"

"Doors open and doors close. Do you doubt God exists in all time considering the places you've been?"

Stephanie didn't answer.

"You didn't question finding yourself as a teenager a few hours ago."

"That seems like days ago."

"In calendar days, it is still today. We haven't left November 22."

"You're having fun with this, aren't you, Carter," Stephanie said, noticing the slight glow of her companion, and it wasn't a halo.

"Very much so. I told my friend I've always desired an assignment like this one. I've heard of them but never talked to an angel who actually had been handed one. Being an avid reader, I am partial to Charles Dickens. *A Christmas Carol* is one of my favorite stories."

Stephanie chewed on his words for a moment. "Does that make you the ghost of Christmas Future right now?"

Carter beamed. "Not at all. For one thing, I am no ghost. And for another, we are still a month away from Christmas."

"But you *are* here to show me the error of my ways. And I have just had one dose of it, haven't I?"

"I don't know. You tell me?"

"If we *are* in the future, I eventually leave Jason. The manager told me I left him five years ago. Jason told the manager I should call my lover if I needed help. *Five years, Carter!* That would be about when I took this trip with Kenneth. What happened that night? I didn't oversleep, did I?"

"There are always two paths to choose in life, Stephanie; two doors you can choose to open. One will lead you down a path of peace. The other will take you down a road that may seem like it will bring you happiness but will end up causing you heartache in the end."

"My life was plain and boring," Stephanie tried to justify herself. "I needed excitement. That's what Kenneth brought to it."

"Stephanie, if anyone knows it, it must be you; you can't have your cake and eat it too. Either you accept that you are a married woman and do what it takes to rekindle your marriage, or you end that marriage and take the chance to pursue a relationship with a man of questionable morals who was bold enough to make advances to a married woman."

"What's that supposed to mean? Kenneth just knew what he wanted and went after it. That's boldness and admirable."

"Ahh. And what if that boldness means he wants more than just you? What if you weren't the only woman he was pursuing? Would you still find that quality admirable? Would it still be attractive to you?

"No. No, Kenneth saw me, and only me. He told me so."

"Did he now?" Carter said, meeting her confused stare.

Stephanie looked up to the ceiling, then out the window.

She wasn't sure if he had said those words, but she was fairly certain that Kenneth only had eyes for her.

Carter stood, grabbed his cup of coffee, and nodded to Stephanie, "Follow me. Let's find a more private area."

Carter led her to the booth where they had been sitting in when he sent her back to her high school days. Stephanie's stomach tumbled in anticipation of another trip.

"Where are you sending me this time, Carter?" Stephanie asked as she sat. The waitress met them, and Carter asked for a refill. Stephanie requested a glass of iced water.

"Where is the Lord sending you, you mean," Carter said. "I don't have control over how God works. I just know He does. Be patient, relax, and allow Him to work."

Carter took her right hand and prayed, "Lord, I know you want to reveal to Stephanie who you are. Open her mind to your teaching. Send her a Little Reminder of who you are."

After Carter's *Amen*, Stephanie opened her eyes, and her water had arrived through a respectful waitress' attention. She sipped on it, drew a deep breath, and released it.

"All I know is this one should be brief," Carter said. "You need to see something before we go further. It will help you understand a few things. It may be emotional, so remain strong and focused until you return, okay?" Carter said, raising his eyebrows.

"That's great for assurance," Stephanie said with a slight laugh. She needed to calm her nerves. She didn't know what to expect. Sitting in the future, knowing she had left her husband, she was sure nothing else could shock her.

"Let's begin," Carter said. He spoke another prayer, similar to the one he said prior to her first trip, only this one wasn't directed to childhood dreams. It was aimed at her virtue and strength of heart. The same fade-to-black imaging swept over her, and the train tunnel reappeared. Her hand covered her eyes until they adjusted. She was back in the 2025 version of the diner. Carter still sat in across from her, sipping a cup of coffee with a short stack in front of him.

"Welcome back, Steph," Carter said, taking a healthy bite.

"Carter? We're still in the diner? What happened? Did it fail?"

"No, not at all. Look outside," Carter nodded.

Stephanie did and was startled to see that it was dark. "Wait, it's nighttime. Where are we? Or I guess a better question is; when are we?"

"It's Friday night. You and Kenneth arrived a few hours ago. As you recall, he went to the desk, checked in, and went upstairs. You followed after he left, checked in, and went to your room. This is where two different outcomes play out. The one where you fall asleep and wake up in the morning with nothing happening. And, of course, there is the alternative."

"So, there is a timeline where I do wake up and go to Kenneth's room?"

"Perhaps. That decision is yours to make," Carter said.

"What are we doing here then, Carter?"

"I want to show you the two instances. Remember, on the beach? You said you were worried about Kenneth and what happened to him?"

"Yes."

"Here is where you get your answer," Carter said.

"Why do I get the feeling I'm not going to like this?"

"Your gut serves you well. But you must understand what you've gotten yourself into. You just told me Kenneth had his eyes set only on you. You must understand the truth."

"You can't just tell me?"

"Would you believe me if I did?"

Stephanie didn't respond.

"Just watch,"

As if on cue, a couple entered the diner. Stephanie's back was to the entrance, but Carter could see them and nodded; Stephanie turned and saw them and stood.

"Wait," Carter admonished her. "There is something you should know about this trip. They can't see or hear you. You're asleep upstairs."

"I need to get closer, so I can hear what they are saying," Stephanie replied.

Carter took another bite and swallowed. "You already know what he is saying. It's the same thing he said to you, only tailored for her."

"I don't understand. He was so sincere. He cared for me," Stephanie said.

"I'm sorry, Stephanie. But you had to see this. You needed to see what Kenneth was truly like."

Stephanie couldn't say a word. She had believed he was interested in her, but it was all a game, bent on getting her down here this weekend. And she had fallen for it. Every step was to get her at that office alone so he could invite her on this trip. Now she was here, and when he couldn't close the deal, he had a backup plan.

"Remain calm, Stephanie. You need to relax so you can return," Carter said. His voice echoed all around her. He was standing in front of her.

Stephanie nodded and took Carter's hand. "Let's just get this over with. Take me back."

Chapter
Sixteen

Saturday, November 22, 2025

Jason had no idea where he was going. He had driven south for the last two hours, heading toward the coast. All he knew was that her client was on the peninsula. He just didn't know where and wasn't even sure if he had the right one. Stephanie had said, *one of their biggest clients.* Vanessa said their biggest was the hotel with a seashell-type name. But also explained that she would know if they were in danger of losing them. Jason felt bad for snapping at her, but he demanded the client's info and ended their call. Now, he was on this adventure, hoping to find her. Hoping because of her Bible that sat on the passenger seat.

Carter had told him that he would know when the right time to talk to Stephanie would be. The moment he saw that Bible, everything clicked, and he knew he needed to find her. Was it God speaking to him? Jason chuckled. That was one thing he hadn't thought about in a while: God. They both had been busy with life and work. Prayer, yeah. But with the kids, the thought of God or church wasn't even a back-burner issue. It made him think about promises made, which now had become promises broken.

Jason always told himself he would never allow work to get in the way of his faith. But with only highway in front of him, he had plenty of time to think. Finding that Bible revealed that this was precisely what he was doing. He worked long hours, came home to pat the kids on the head and kiss Stephanie on the cheek, then turned on the TV to zone out to whatever game was on until bedtime. Somewhere in there, he ate. Funny, he didn't remember where dinner came from. Maybe Stephanie made it. Maybe she brought home takeout. He just didn't know. *Have I really become that disconnected?*

"God, what have I done," Jason spoke to the heavens and the steering wheel.

Is that what Carter was telling him? Jason was trying to understand how Carter could know so much about his and Stephanie's relationship. *The guy said God sent him.* Jason shook his head. *Insane! If only I had more time with him. Maybe he knew where Stephanie is right now. He did say she was safe, though. That's something.*

But for some reason, he knew a piece was missing—call it a husband's intuition—and he knew he needed to find her.

Jason pushed his vehicle a bit faster, checking his mirrors for safety. He didn't see any recognizable headlights or any glow of red idling on the side of the highway. His heart thumped in his chest, and he could feel the steering wheel slicken under his hands. A highway sign lit up under his high beams: Wilmington 60 mi. Jason sighed. Still another hour.

Jason clicked a steering wheel button and said, "Satellite Maps. Search for hotels in Wilmington, North Carolina."

"Too many to list. Please narrow your search parameters," the female voice said.

"List hotels South of Highway 117," Jason said.

"Working," the navigator said. "There are 74 locations, including hotels, motels, and rest areas for your convenience."

Jason shook his head. *Getting closer*. He quick-glanced at the map the navigator was showing him. He tapped to zoom in. He remembered that Vanessa had said something about shells.

"Satellite Maps. Find a motel on the peninsula with shells in its name."

"Processing."

Jason shook his head and mumbled, "There can't be that many."

"I have three possible locations. Shells Motel and Eatery on Highway 421 in Silver Lake; Beautiful Shells by the Sea Resort in Kure Beach; and Sand Dollar Condos on Sea Shell lane in Carolina Beach."

"That's it!" Jason yelled at the navigation system. "Please navigate to Sand Dollar Condos."

"Processing," the computer said.

Jason was confident that was the place. The moment he heard *sand dollar*, the memories returned. It was her first breakthrough client and a sign of what was to come—all because of their walk on Myrtle Beach when he picked up that sand dollar. He could understand the connection. He made promises that day. *Was this the client that was leaving her? Was this why she was so desperate to keep them that she had to rush down here?*

"You will reach your destination in fifty-five minutes on your current route. Would you care for me to suggest an alternate route, Mr. Marshall, that would save you five minutes?"

While Jason was one for saving time, taking a highway in the dark that a computer suggested was not for him at the moment. "No. Keep me on the current route, thank you."

"You will reach your destination in fifty-four minutes," the computer binged and then returned to the instrumental jazz it had been playing.

Within an hour, Jason pulled up to a rock waterfall and an illuminated sign welcoming him to Sand Dollar Condos.

"You have reached your destination," his car congratulated him.

Jason cruised the front of the complex. There was a gate along the front of the community which required a passcode. He couldn't see an office from where he was, just a directional sign assuring him it was *that way.*

"Now what, Jason?" he said aloud as he circled the cul-de-sac. A yellow light on the dash grabbed his attention. *Low fuel.*

"Dang it," he muttered. He remembered seeing a station just before he turned off the highway. He figured there was nothing more he could do here. He turned around and headed back.

The station, situated at the top of a hill, was welcoming. The sea breeze wafted the ocean air around the pumps, taking Jason back to the day he found the shell. He remembered walking and avoiding Stephanie's eye contact. Why he was nervous was beyond him. He was a grown man, but she had that effect on him. He spent most of the time eying the ground, counting shells. Until one of them stood out; it was a sand dollar. He picked it up, allowed a wave to rinse it off, then gave it to Stephanie. Both of them soon realized its uniqueness, the one eye. Jason smiled at the memory, then frowned. He remembered they were saddened when they found it broken in Joshua's room, the result of an innocent child's curiosity, not knowing what he held.

The handle clicked under Jason's hand, and he gave it one last squeeze to be sure, then twisted the cap back on and replaced the nozzle in the receptacle. The machine screen flashed, DO YOU WANT A RECEIPT? Jason read it, then re-read it. He felt dumb for not realizing it sooner—*a receipt!* Stephanie would've made a reservation, and the address of where she was staying would be on that charge.

Jason hit 'no,' completing his purchase and stepped into his truck. He checked his banking app, but there were no hotel or other charges in the last forty-eight hours. Jason couldn't understand. How could there be nothing? *Unless…* it frustrated him to realize he would have to make another call to Vanessa.

The phone rang, and she answered with a not happy to be answering a call after nine PM voice.

"Hello, Jason. What can I do for you?"

"Hi, Vanessa." Jason began. "Yes, I know it's late, but I need your help again. I'm down here at Sand Dollar Condos."

"You actually went?"

"Yes. The office is closed, and I don't know where Stephanie is. But I need to find her tonight. Did she tell you where she was staying? Or do you have access to the company charge account to look up recent activity?"

"Look, Jason," Vanessa began.

"Please, Vanessa. I need to fix things with her. I hope I'm not too late for that. It's why I made this trip. I don't know what to expect when I find her, but I'm willing to take that risk. I don't know. I just have a sick feeling."

There was silence over the phone.

"Are you there? Vanessa? I just need to find out which hotel she's at, and I don't want to knock on the door of seventy-two hotel rooms."

Jason heard a sigh, but he could also hear keystrokes. "Recent activity shows she purchased a single room at Hotel by the Sea. It's on Highway 421. Oh, hell."

"What?"

"Nothing," Vanessa said. "You can find the hotel on the main highway; it is seaside."

"Vanessa, what are you hiding? Don't lie to me."

"It could be nothing, really."

"Just tell me already, Vanessa?"

"We all have corporate cards. It's for when we conduct business with a client, like having lunch or other out-of-town business expenses. Like this trip was to meet with a business client."

"Cut to the chase, please."

"It could be a bank error, but the account has been flagged because, within fifteen minutes, there were duplicate purchases for a room at the same location."

"So, there was a mistake in billing. Why the dismay?"

"The rooms were purchased with two different card numbers," Vanessa explained. "While the company has one account, each of us has our own card to identify our expenses. Keeps us honest."

"So, there is no bank error, and someone is down here with my wife?"

"Jason, I wouldn't go jumping to conclusions. There could be any number of reasons this could be happening?"

"Name one?"

Vanessa was silent.

"Who is she down here with, Vanessa?"

"I believe the second charge belongs to Kenneth Alistair."

Sunday, November 24, 2030

Stephanie opened her eyes. It was dark and cold. The ground had a light covering of snow. It reminded her of that first snowfall of the season, not that North Carolina received a great deal of the white stuff. But this was not Carolina; she could feel it. Where was she? *When* was she? With the sun gone, she couldn't judge the time, much less the date.

"Carter? Where did you go?" Stephanie was grateful for the lack of a post time traversing hangover this time. But not knowing where she was made her nervous. She took a deep breath, remembering Carter's warning to remain calm and focused. If she was here to accomplish something, she needed to find and complete that mission. The problem was, the hotel was nowhere to be seen, nor was there any scent of the ocean nearby. She did notice the smell of gas and city tar.

"We're definitely not in North Carolina anymore, Stephanie," she said to no one, or so she thought.

"Nope," said a voice that belonged to a man who was approaching her. "You're in Texas, ma'am. Houston, to be exact. If you're here for the meal, that doesn't happen for another few days."

"The meal?"

"The meal for the homeless," the man said.

"I will have you know I am anything but homeless," Stephanie snapped, rubbing her arms.

"I apologize," the man stepped back, hands surrendered. "I didn't see your car. With weather like this, I wouldn't think anyone would choose to walk in it."

Stephanie looked around, the streets were empty, and the narrow road was void of cars. She did seem out of place. "My car is on the highway. I broke down and saw the sign," she said, knowing that no one could really see the sign from the main road. She hadn't even noticed it until the man had addressed her.

"Mmm-kay. Well, we're closed, but I can let you in to make a phone call if you'd like. I'll even make you a cup of coffee and offer you a slice of pie. I'm here to finish an article. I needed to get away from everything for a while, if you know what I mean."

Stephanie snorted. "Yeah, I suppose. I could go for getting out of the cold."

They walked to the building, which looked like a double-wide mobile-home but had a sign that read Davie's Deli above the roof.

"Davie's Deli?" Stephanie said. The name seemed familiar, but she couldn't place it. "This doesn't look like a restaurant."

The man laughed. "That's what everyone says. It's how Mom and Pop designed it. They wanted everyone to feel like they were coming home to eat while still going out."

"Genius," Stephanie said, taking in the rest of her surroundings. "Does it bring in much business?"

"And how. It's one of Houston's hidden gems," the man said, unlocking the door.

"Are you the manager?"

"In a sense. I'm the owner," the man said, his voice suddenly heavy. "Come on in, and I'll tell you all about it. My name is Aaron Stephenson." He extending his gloved hand, and Stephanie accepted it with a bare, cold hand. When their hands met, though, Stephanie's memory was triggered. She looked at the sign again, then back to Aaron—*Carter's friend, Aaron.*

"Nice to meet you, Aaron. I'm Stephanie. I hope you have cocoa in there," she said with a laugh.

"For you, I will make a cup of cocoa that'll make your head spin. It was my wife's favorite." He locked the door behind them, turning on the small run of lights that flickered then lit up the front counter.

"What in the world?" Stephanie was in awe seeing the teal, black, and white decor. *Carter said this place was unique, that was by far an understatement.* "You have to be kidding me? Whose idea was the retro theme?"

"That was Mom. She always loved the soda shops she grew up with. Pop loved mom, so they modeled everything after their childhood."

"Mom had excellent taste."

"That she did. She passed away about six years ago. And I was nervous for Pop. I thought he might close the place up. But it only ignited his fire. He pressed on, and we continued with the restaurant and the traditions."

"Traditions?"

"You must not be a local," Aaron said, turning on the coffee maker.

"No, sorry, I'm not."

"South Carolina, that's right. You were mumbling outside."

"North Carolina, thank you."

"My apologies. *North* Carolina. Well, North Carolina, Davies Deli is well-known around Houston for two things. The first is for its Meatloaf Sandwich."

"You have got to be joking? Meatloaf? Sandwich?" Stephanie wrinkled her nose. *Carter wasn't joking. This was the place.*

"Hey, don't turn your nose up at it until you try it. You'll change your tune once you've tasted Pop's special recipe. Most people do, and we usually have a line waiting to get in. Writers clamor to write a piece on it from border to border."

Stephanie laughed.

"Did I miss something?" Aaron asked.

"I just happen to be a writer, and I don't believe I've heard of a meatloaf sandwich," Stephanie said. Well, she hadn't heard of it until her recent encounter.

"*Hmmph*," Aaron said, scratching his chin and looking her over.

"I know, I know. How can a woman who just walked in off the street be a writer? Just trust me. I am a freelance writer from Charlotte, North Carolina."

"Uh-huh. Charlotte, North Carolina?" Aaron said. "What is your full name, Stephanie?"

"Stephanie Marshall. I own Marshall Copywriting in Evansville, North Carolina."

"Mmhmm. So not Charlotte? Doesn't matter. The name sounds familiar, though," Aaron said.

"Ahahaa. So, you have *heard* of me," Stephanie said. "See, this medium-sized business from a small city does make an impact up here in the Lone Star State."

"But I can't place it," Aaron finished his statement.

"Regardless, you know my name."

The room began to percolate with the aroma of coffee, and Stephanie felt as if she belonged there. Was this part of Carter's doing or the reality of being in Davies Deli, just as he spoke of? "This place sure does draw you in. It is welcoming. I will have to write about it when I get back home."

"I'd appreciate it. Charlotte, or Evansville, will have a place to travel to now," Aaron said. He set two cups on the counter, filled one with coffee and the other with hot cocoa. "We've had people as far north as Denver and as far west as San Diego come in to try our food and write a review. Especially with the Thanksgiving event. It will be great to grab a few East Coasters."

"My pleasure," Stephanie sipped her cup. "You said something about having to write a paper?"

"Yes. You and I share a common goal. To appease the readership of America."

"So, *you are* a writer? What's with the restaurant?"

"I am a jack of all trades," Aaron explained, waving his hand around the room. "I run the restaurant by day and write when I'm supposed to be sleeping."

"Ahh, thus the three AM writing call."

Aaron laughed. "Exactly."

"So, are you a freelancer, or are you tied to a desk?"

"Both, in a way," Aaron explained. "I write a column for a local periodical; then I accept freelance work as needed. They know about the restaurant, so they give me the freedom to work remotely."

"But what about Pop? Where is he?" Stephanie asked.

Aaron began to tear up.

"I'm sorry. Did I say something wrong?"

"Pop passed away last week."

"I'm so sorry, Aaron. I don't know what to say." Stephanie wasn't sure what to do. Aaron looked like he needed a shoulder, but she wasn't sure she could make such an advance after having only just met the man.

"Don't be," Aaron wiped his eyes. "Sorry, I don't mean to be emotional. It's all so recent, and I'm still adjusting. I am sad about this loss, but he is in a better place. I'm also happy that he kept up until the end. He died doing the thing he loved. He literally died with a spatula in his hand." Aaron smiled.

Stephanie slowly looked toward the kitchen with a puzzled look.

Aaron had to laugh, stopping his tears. "No, it wasn't here. He has a kitchen at home. We were there planning for this year's Thanksgiving Event."

"Tell me about that, it's the third time you've mentioned it."

"Ah yes, *the event*," Aaron said in a lower octave. "We hold an annual Thanksgiving meal where we feed the homeless in the area. We've held it for going on ten years now. But with Pop gone, I'm contemplating canceling it this year. I can't do it on my own. Pop was always the fire that kindled that kitchen to success."

"I don't understand."

"Our first Thanksgiving meal, we fed about three hundred people. By our fifth year we were feeding fifteen hundred. Last year we fed just over two thousand."

"You have got to be kidding me?"

"Not at all. God has blessed us with the ability and the funding to get it all done."

"From this tiny establishment?"

"Yep."

"Two thousand? From where?"

"I have no clue, Stephanie. Homeless, nurses, office clerks, city workers, plumbers, clergy—all kinds come here to be fed. We had originally planned to feed the homeless, but it just blew up from there. Mind you, we don't turn away anyone in place of another. It is amazing, Stephanie. I've seen the homeless sitting across from an attorney holding a civil conversation. The same people you see turn away from each other on the street. God does amazing things here. But that was Pop's thing. And now he's gone." Aaron's tears returned. "How am I supposed to continue this alone? I don't have what it takes. I can't do it. I just can't."

Stephanie watched as Aaron bore the load of defeat. She also recalled Carter's words and the joy he received from this place. *If a small eatery could bring joy to an angel of the Lord, how much more does it bring to everyone else that walks through those doors?* Maybe Aaron needed a little encouragement from someone at the right moment to give him a Little Reminder. Perhaps she was sent here to give him that boost. But she also knew that *she* was here for a reason. What did Aaron have for her? That remained to be seen.

Chapter
Seventeen

Saturday, November 22, 2025

Jason didn't want to believe what he had heard. But Vanessa's tone said it all. Her doubt was evident. Her attempt to cover it up was a clear indicator. Vanessa reluctantly gave him the address to the Hotel by the Sea, not that it mattered. It would be easy to find on his own. It was only a matter of time now.

It turned out it was less than a mile from his current location. It made him wonder if that was the reason she chose it. It also pained him because it allowed his mind to wander to his wife walking the beach with Kenneth as they had. *Did they walk together to a meeting with the manager? Were they holding hands and making memories, perhaps finding sand dollars of their own?* Jason had to shake the thoughts from his head. He was losing focus on the road and beginning to see red.

"How could you do this to us, Steph?" he said to the steering wheel. "How could you do this to our family?"

He knew he hadn't been the perfect husband, but he never thought he had pushed her away. *Was that the reason she was staying late at work? Were those really late meetings, or was it more—* Bright headlights and a horn blaring jarred Jason out of his thoughts again, and this time he had to swerve back into his lane. His heart pounded. He pulled into the next entrance and parked.

"What am I going to do, Lord?" Jason prayed. Then the tears began to fall.

Jason was startled by a tap on his window. "You okay, mister?" A voice called to him.

He looked up at a figure in the dark parking lot. He turned on the dome light and rolled down his window. "Yeah, I'm fine. I just needed to stop for a minute. I'm a bit lost. I was going to check my GPS. Give me a second, and I will be out of your way. Sorry if I've intruded."

"You're fine. Can I help you find something? I don't know the area all that well—my fiancée and I are visiting ourselves—but I can try to help. We were coming out of the church and saw you sitting here. Just wanted to make sure you were okay."

"Church? I didn't see a church on the peninsula coming in?"

"It's a community center. No signage yet. They have banners inside, though. You can go in if you'd like. They are having a meal. I'm sure they would welcome a visitor."

Jason looked at the building. He felt pulled to go inside. He knew finding his wife was crucial, but the church and the offer from the gentleman were hard to resist. "I think I may just do that."

"Great. Well, I need to get going. We need to get back to our hotel and get some rest. Heading back to Texas tomorrow. My name is Derrick," the man extended his hand. "This is my fiancée, Breonna."

"I'm Jason." He shook Derrick's hand and tipped an imaginary hat toward Breonna. "Good evening."

"Good evening," Breonna said, giving him one of the brightest smiles he'd ever seen.

The two left him to find their vehicle in the darkened lot, disagreeing on where he parked it, comparing the lights to the strip mall they worked at. Jason laughed, remembering the bickering he and Stephanie would get into about the small things. It was those things he missed most. Now they didn't seem to talk about much of anything. He would welcome a minor spat. He knew he was equally at fault. It wasn't like he went out of his way to communicate with her, especially when a game was on. And yeah, he could blame it on being worn out from a hard day at work, but that was just making excuses.

Jason stepped out of his truck and made his way across the parking lot. *Derrick was right, it is dark out. I wonder why the community center doesn't add some lighting?* But the front door lights were doing their job, drawing him forward with their welcoming glow. There were people in the lobby conversing in groups. *Church-going folk,* he thought. They weren't dressed up, but they weren't dressed down either. He looked down at his jeans, boots, and button-up. *It'll have to do,* he thought.

The door made an aluminum scraping sound as he entered, and two of the groups turned their attention to him. One, a fatherly gentleman, spoke. "May I help you?"

"I was out in my truck, and Derrick said I should come inside. My name is Jason."

"Jason. Hello, I am Pastor Elliot." He extended his hand.

"Good evening," Jason said, accepting the greeting.

"Are you hungry? There's plenty of food back here. I'm sure

that's why Derrick sent you in. He *always* has food on his mind." The pastor let out a hearty laugh.

"Sure, I could eat something. I've been driving for so long I forgot to eat this evening."

"Driving? Where are you coming from?"

"Charlotte," Jason said, then grew nervous that he would have to tell his story. He knew how ministers liked to play twenty questions. He followed him to the serving line, ready to follow along with whatever questions came next.

"Ahh. I have a sister up there. She loves it. I don't get to see her as much as I'd like to, though."

"Sorry to hear that," Jason responded, unsure what else to say. The pastor took a plate, and Jason followed suit. The variety of food was amazed. Everything he could imagine was lined out before him. "Wow, this is some spread."

"Yes, our members go all out. If anyone goes away hungry, it's their own fault." Pastor Elliot began to pile on his plate, and Jason followed.

"You haven't eaten yet?" Jason asked.

"No. I try and make sure everyone else eats before I do. Don't want to take something that someone else would want."

"Well, I'm honored to eat with you, then." Jason piled on whatever he saw. Sausage, chicken, all varieties of vegetable concoctions—everything looked good.

"The honor is mine. I'm glad you found us. May I sit with you?"

"I would like that. I don't know anyone," Jason said.

"Wonderful," the pastor directed him to a table.

"I don't have much time, though. I wasn't planning to stop until Derrick grabbed me."

"Got someplace to be?"

Jason nodded with a mouthful, then swallowed. "I'm looking for Hotel by the Sea. I have a reservation. Didn't see it on the way in, and I think I may have passed it. It's my first time on the peninsula, and I didn't mean to come down here so late." He hated to lie to a pastor, but he didn't want to reveal the truth. He wasn't ready for the lecture that he was sure would follow. *Tell the pastor that I'm searching for my wife, who may or may not have run off with another man? I don't think so.*

"Ahh, yes. That hotel is just on the other side of the light—thataway," the pastor pointed to the wall.

"That's great. I don't have too far to go then." Jason felt a sudden rise of anxiety and stopped eating. He was about a football field away from his wife. He shook his head. *Another sports analogy? Yeesh! No wonder Stephanie doesn't talk to me.*

"You okay?" Pastor Elliot asked, catching his distraction.

"Yeah, sorry, lost focus there for a moment."

"Forgive me, but I'm sensing there may be more to your story than you are letting on."

"I will be honest with you, Pastor Elliot," Jason began before he even had time to think about his response. "I'm not on vacation. I *am* from Charlotte, but I came here because I'm following my wife. I believe she is at that hotel with another man."

Why is it so easy to talk to this stranger? Whatever the reason, Jason discovered that releasing what he held inside helped. He didn't cry about it. He had cried all of his tears on the three-hour drive down here. Now, sitting a block away from the hotel, he feared the reality of the moment. The confusion of what to do next left his legs numb. His confession gave him a sense of calm. It didn't solve his problem, but he felt more focused than he had been since he started this journey.

"I appreciate you sharing this with me, Jason. I'm sorry this is happening to you. But I'm glad you found us. God must've turned your vehicle at just the right time."

"Heh. I would blame that on a set of headlights that nearly hit me head-on," Jason laughed. "But I understand your meaning."

"God doesn't allow anything to happen by accident, no pun intended. He had His hand on you. No matter what happens with you and your wife, He knows your situation and will guide you through it if you ask Him. May I ask if you are a Christian, Jason?"

Jason gritted his teeth and rocked his head. "I thought I was—once. I guess life just got so busy. It's not that I don't believe in God; I do. But I just haven't had the time..." his voice trailed off.

"Can I ask you a personal question?"

"I have revealed so much to you so far, why not? Shoot."

"Has your wife fallen into that category as well?"

"How do you mean?"

"You said that you've been too busy for God, but still believe in Him. Does that apply to your wife as well? Has your life been so busy that, well—and it's not that you don't love her, but you just don't have *time* for *her*?"

Jason felt like a knife had just pierced his heart. It confirmed all he had been thinking on the road. But hearing it from someone else somehow hit him harder. He didn't think he had any tears left in him. He was wrong. Embarrassed, he glanced around the room, but no one paid much attention—it was just him and the pastor.

"It's okay." Pastor Elliot's voice took on a soothing tone. "You'll be okay, Jason. You just need to find what's broken and decide to fix it. So, what do you do for a living?"

Jason wiped his cheek with his sleeve and gave a half-laugh. "I'm a carpenter. I build homes for a living."

"Ha!" exclaimed the pastor. "There you go. You understand more than most folks about putting things together. If something isn't lining up, you must find what's wrong before moving on to the next step. Building a solid marriage is a lot like building a home. If the foundation is solid, pretty much everything else can be fixed. I'm not saying it won't take work, but it looks to me like you're a man who isn't afraid of hard work."

Jason nodded. The pastor was right. He knew there were things in his own life he needed to change, and he was willing to do whatever it took to make it right. And this stop helped him see that.

"Can I pray with you, Jason?"

"I would like that."

The pastor's prayer reminded Jason he was not where he needed to be with God. It had been a long time since he cracked open a Bible. It had been even longer since he had attended a church service. When he and Stephanie got married, it had been a routine practice, but somewhere between *just this one time* and *I'm too tired for church today*, his relationship with God was lost in the business of life. He felt sure Stephanie could say the same thing. Was she experiencing the same issues with God in her life? Perhaps this affair was part of it?

After the pastor's "Amen," he and Jason talked about other subjects, such as the church's future and how the growing congregation aspired to move from the convention hall into a permanent structure. Jason shared his ideas for saving costs and even handed him a card for when he had funding to take the next step.

With the meal past, the pastor walked Jason to his truck, pointed him toward the hotel, waved goodbye, then walked back into the hall where he greeted another new face. This one had a stubbly white beard and wore a coat and matching tweet hat.

"Welcome, friend," the pastor said. "Are you hungry?"

Chapter
Eighteen

Sunday, November 24, 2030

After a couple of cups of coffee and sharing a few stories of articles they had written, Stephanie felt comfortable with Aaron. They were kindred spirits, as writers usually are. They shared similar stories about how they got started—small pieces with their school paper that developed into local newspaper article. Aaron was impressed with how bold she was at taking it to the next level in starting her own business. He mentioned how he had dreamed of going full time freelance but never had the guts to do it. Then the restaurateur in him took over, or rather, the restaurant took *him* over.

"Writing can be an amazing tool to reach people's souls," Stephanie said. "My high school journalism teacher taught me that."

Aaron laughed. "It definitely can grab their attention and convince them to make decisions they would not normally make. Meaning you can change a person's mind with words if you know how to use them."

"Most definitely," Stephanie agreed, raising her cocoa cup.

Aaron met it; the clanging echoed through the empty restaurant.

"So, this place really does that well?" Stephanie again felt the swooning charm of Davie's Deli. Carter was right, this place was a home away from home. No wonder angels were lining up to experience a heavenly place like this one.

"It does. Every day. Day in and day out. Pop created a buzz about the place by introducing a daily special. Each day has its own special sandwich. I've already told you about the meatloaf sandwich."

"What about today? What would today's special be?"

"Well, today is Sunday, so we are closed. We don't work on the Lord's Day."

Stephanie nodded. "I can respect that. So, you are a Christian?"

"Yes, ma'am. I couldn't make it without God on my side. He has seen me through so much, especially with this place."

"How so?"

"About ten years ago, I met Pop's daughter. Her name was Deborah..."

"Was? Oh my," Stephanie said, clasping her mouth. "Sorry, I think I can see where this is going. I'm so, so sorry..."

"It's okay. I'm okay." Aaron smiled. "Deborah was amazing. She did the books here for Pop."

"How did you meet?"

Aaron laughed. "How else? I was a customer. Well, I was also a writer on assignment for a story on *the deli with the funny sandwiches*." He made air quotes with his finger. "This was when the meatloaf sandwich first hit the spotlight. Most of this wasn't here," Aaron pointed to the kitchen. "Pop added on after the popularity explosion.

"I had one sandwich and was hooked. Truth be told, I was also hooked on the beautiful woman with the messy ponytail who just happened to be Pop's daughter. She not only did the books but filled in as a waitress when needed. I eventually built up the nerve to ask her out. We dated for a while, but she was diagnosed with an inoperable tumor. When they operated, there were complications, and she died during surgery."

"Wow, Aaron. I'm so sorry."

"Really, It's okay. It was a long time ago. I've come to accept it."

"How long did you know her before she passed away?"

"Not long, but it seemed like forever. The anniversary of her passing is this week."

"She died during the Thanksgiving holiday?"

"Yeah," Aaron said softly. "Deborah, DeeDee as Pop called her, had always wanted to do something for the community. To make a long story short, Deborah was pulling in donations from all over to orchestrate the first community Thanksgiving dinner here. We almost didn't have it because of her passing, but one morning I stopped by, and Pop was feverishly working in the kitchen, prepping. He asked why in the world we wouldn't have it. It would disrespect his daughter's memory, and she would be upset with both of us if we didn't have it."

Stephanie laughed. "I would assume so. If she was the fighter you say she was, I would think all the work she put into it would be for nothing; I'd be upset too."

"Yeah. So, we pulled everyone together and served about three hundred people that first Thanksgiving."

"And you are considering quitting again?"

"I can't do this without Pop. He was the one who convinced me to continue when we lost Deborah."

"And I bet you were the one who convinced him to continue when he lost Mom?"

Aaron seemed lost in thought for a moment. "In a way. He slowed down for a bit, but we lost her in May. He had plenty of time to recuperate before November."

"I get that, but it still must've been difficult."

"True. But Pop is—*was*—the one who kept all of this going. Now I don't know how to finish. I have been so focused on Thanksgiving; I haven't even considered the restaurant itself. I'm a writer. I can rate a restaurant all day; I can't run one—not by myself. I am a food connoisseur; not a kitchen manager."

"I'm sure that God will provide for you. You said you couldn't make it without God on your side. Well, if He didn't leave your side before, what makes you think He has left your side now?"

Where did those words come from? Stephanie wondered. *I don't even remember the last time I talked to God, much less about Him.*

"Sorry. Listen to me talking about something I know absolutely nothing about. I don't even know how to manage my own life, and here I am, giving Godly instructions to another person. I'm starting to sound like a certain tweed-hatted fellow with a prepotency for giving life advice," Stephanie said.

Aaron stared at her, wide-eyed stare, his hand lowering his coffee mug. "Tweed hat? Did you just say *tweed hat—with a matching coat?*"

"Yeah. But you probably don't remember the guy. He is someone who 1 know from back home who mentioned..."

"You would be surprised how many people I remember, Stephanie," Aaron said. "Especially those who wear a tweed hat and matching coat."

Stephanie couldn't believe what she had just heard. She hadn't mentioned the coat. "You know who I'm talking about?"

Aaron nodded. "Carter Jennings is a man you don't soon forget."

Saturday, November 22, 2025

Jason cruised the small parking lot for the third time. There was no sign of Stephanie's car. Even though it was dark, he could differentiate the make and model of the vehicles. None of them were his wife's. Either she was still out on the town with her paramour, or she was staying at a different hotel. He wondered if he would be able to get any information from a sympathetic hotel manager.

A security SUV drove past him for the second time. He needed to either move on or park and go inside, or he might have some explaining to do with law enforcement.

I could always head inside. It looked as if there was a restaurant. Maybe they have late hours. But what if they are inside, and her car is parked somewhere else? What if they left her car at his place, and she rode down here in his car?

He couldn't go inside. His stomach sank again with the thought of them sharing memories of a car trip.

Jason pulled out of the hotel parking lot and drove to a nearby a convenience store. He used the facilities and grabbed a soft drink, then drove around until he found a spot to park that gave him an unobstructed view of the hotel—and waited.

He felt guilty about stalking his wife, but he didn't know what else to do. After an hour he admitted he wasn't cut out for working a stake-out. He didn't know how cops did it. He was tired, fed up, and needed to use the restroom again. Rather than driving back to the convenience store, he chose to drive to the hotel. Having to use the facilities would give him a reason to go inside without looking look like a fool.

Once inside the hotel, Jason saw the restaurant idea was out of the question; it was closed. But at the other end of the lobby, there appeared to be an entrance to a bar. There was a door with a glowing neon sign. Jason found the restroom, fixed his full bladder issue, and headed toward the green and red glow.

The sign wasn't fancy, just a red and green glow that read Lounge with an entrance around a corner. Nervous about what he might find, he took a breath.

He tried to remember what Kenneth looked like. Dark hair. That was it. That was all he could remember about the guy. *Not particularly helpful*, he muttered under his breath. *It only applies to about three-quarters of the population.* But he figured it he saw a guy with a smug look on his face sitting next to his wife, that would be the guy.

Jason said a quick prayer before opening the door. The lounge was much larger than he expected. It was lit up much like the sign, neon, but in blues and reds. The bar itself was to his right, along the wall. The room held a smattering of people, mostly small groups. There were two tables with couples. Neither of them included his wife.

An empty stool at the bar opened up, and Jason walked up to it and sat.

"What will ya have?" the bartender asked.

"Sarsaparilla?" Jason jested.

The bartender rolled her eyes. "Funny," she said. "I haven't heard that one...today."

"Sorry. Dos Equis. Bottle. Dressed."

The tender nodded and returned a few seconds later with his beer. Not much of a drinker, Jason nursed the bottle. *When in Rome*, he reasoned. Plus, if he wanted to get information, he needed to look like a patron than a jealous husband. He wasn't even sure how to bring it up in the first place. This wasn't like a television show where the hero showed a photo around and people started giving information. Or was it?

Jason pulled up a photo of Stephanie on his phone and turned to the bartender. "Excuse me. Have you seen this woman in here?"

The bartender shook her head.

Jason nodded and bit the corner of his mouth. "I get ya." He took out his wallet, pulled out a twenty, and dropped it in the tip jar. "How about now?"

"Sir, I appreciate the tip, but I haven't seen this woman in here. I do hope you find her," the bartender smiled wide. Jason could tell she wanted to laugh at his antics. He could also tell she was telling the truth. Stephanie had not been in the bar.

With egg on his face, Jason sat back and sulked into his beer. After a couple more sips, a raucous incident developed behind him. Someone with some obvious clout had entered the room. Everyone was calling on him like they were on an episode of *Cheers*.

"Mr. Alistair, welcome back," said one of the waitresses.

"Yes, Mr. Alistair, it is good to see you again," the bartender said.

"Now, Audrey. How many times have I told you, my father is Mr. Alistair. Call me Kenneth."

Jason could see Audrey shaking her head. He couldn't tell if she was annoyed or flattered.

"Well then, good evening, *Kenneth*. Welcome back. I see you have company this evening. What will you two be having?"

Chapter
Nineteen

Sunday, November 24, 2030

"How in the world do you know Carter Jennings?" Stephanie said. "He said he had been a customer here, but—you know him personally? How?"

"That is a long story," Aaron said. "One I can't share with you. Carter is a rather private individual."

"I already know he is an angel. He says he's on a mission from God to save my soul," Stephanie said, still unconvinced.

Aaron nodded. Stephanie was trying to read his reaction to see what it would reveal about his interaction with Carter. "Out of respect for my friend, I still can't go into much detail other than you can trust whatever he tells you. He is an honest… he is honest."

Aaron's pause tipped his hand. She didn't want to call him on it. Yet. "I can accept that. So, you have known him for a while, then?"

"Let's just say I have known him as long as I've known Deborah and leave it at that," Aaron said.

Stephanie nodded. "So, ten years. Since 2015."

"No ten years. Since 2020."

Stephanie gave Aaron a confused look. "Wait, what? No, ten years ago would be 2015."

"Stephanie, it's 2030. What year do you think it is?"

"It's 2025."

Stephanie almost slipped out of her seat. "That Carter."

"You mean?"

"Ever since I met him, he has been slipping me in and out of time," Stephanie revealed.

Aaron grunted, "Well, that's a new one."

"New one?" Stephanie asked. "You know about this?"

"Okay, I'll be straight with you. Yes, Carter is an angel sent by God. He helps people. But I have never known him, or God, to intervene with time." Aaron began to look Stephanie over with new curiosity.

"What? Stop that! What are you doing?"

"Are you really from 2025?"

"Yes. Now stop looking at me like that. If anyone should be staring, it should be me. You're the one from the future."

"True," Aaron said. He looked around the deli.

"Now what?" Stephanie followed his glances.

"I'm trying to remember what this place looked like five years ago. I don't think we've done anything significant besides touch up the paint. And repair some felt on a booth or two."

"So why me? What did I do that God picked me?"

"I don't know. But I do know that God has His reasons. In my case, Carter wasn't sent to help me—he was sent for Deborah. She was wavering in her faith. Carter was sent to give her Little Reminders to bring her back into a right relationship with God."

"Little Reminders?"

"Yeah. Little Reminders. Things that remind us of who we once were. They can be anything. A knick-knack, an old heirloom—in Deborah's case, I found an old Bible that belonged to her at a flea market. It was the strangest thing, too. There was no reason for the Bible to be there, but it was. And we are convinced that God placed it there for me to find."

"You mean Deborah found things, these Little Reminders, out of place, that took her back to her past?"

"Yeah, exactly. And let me guess. You have been finding Little Reminders. How many so far?"

"Three, if you count the menu. Carter handed it to me himself," Stephanie said.

"Another first," Aaron said. "Well, after our last encounter, I would believe anything."

"Your last encounter? You have seen him more than once?"

Aaron laughed. "Yes, but that, too, is a long story. And one I *will* keep to myself. I'll just say that Carter helps people like you who are struggling to find themselves. If he is assigned to you, you should search your heart, listen to his advice, and pray... pray above all things, and seek God. God is most important. Then take in all the Little Reminders you find; they will lead you to your resolution."

Stephanie couldn't believe she was sitting with someone who'd had not one but two encounters with Carter Jennings. She remembered Carter talking about Texas. And this was the place he spoke so fondly of?

"Carter spoke of you and Davies Deli. He said something about south Texas and a deli that served amazing sandwiches."

"Did he now?" Aaron's face lit up like a proud father.

"Would be a shame to close down a place that heavenly beings descend the stairway to heaven to eat at."

"Nice try, but Carter is earthbound. He stays here to help people like you and me."

"How do you know this?"

"I told you, we are close. I would call him a brother or an uncle. He comes in and eats whenever he is in town," Aaron pointed to the counter, "sits right there."

"You are kidding me," Stephanie slugged Aaron's arm.

"No, I am not," Aaron said, laughing. "I would write about it, but I don't think Gabriel would like it.

"Gabriel?"

"Oops. Never mind. Forget I said that name."

"No! Too late. I want to know about it."

"No, really. Forget about it. I went too far there," Aaron extended his hand. "Carter would have my neck if he knew I had said anything about his boss."

Stephanie nodded, accepting his explanation. She understood about a writer's source, and if Aaron was asked to keep a source under wraps, it must mean something.

"Now I wish I could write about you," Aaron said, then paused. "Oh, man…"

"What?" Stephanie said.

"I think I just remembered where I heard your name before," Aaron reached into his bag for his laptop.

Stephanie's nervousness returned. She already knew about her divorce. How much worse could it get if a man in South Texas knew her name? She waited as his laptop booted up.

He didn't waste time and searched for her name. "I knew it. You are Stephanie Ann Marshall of Evansville, North Carolina, correct?'

Reluctantly Stephanie uttered, "Yeah."

Arron skim reads, "You lost your business four years ago for

plagiarism and fraud. Apparently, The Sand Dollar Condos'
parent company sued you for false statements you made
about their complex and breach of contract. They won a 2.3
million-dollar case. Your business folded a week later."

"That...can't be true."

Stephanie slid beside him and Aaron clicked on a link,
bringing up one of the stories.

*CHARLOTTE TIMES: October 12, 2026,
Local news columnist and business owner
Stephanie Ann Marshall was indicted on
fraud charges this week against the
McManus Corporation. Gerald McManus,
CEO and owner of The Sand Dollar Condominium complex in Carolina Beach,
claims that Marshall made false statements in her advertising that could
cause a loss of business to the complex attuned to tens of thousands of
dollars. His claim is that Marshall
did irreparable damage to his brand
that over the course of years, the
loss of funds his company could suffer,
would cause him to lower rental rates.
The judge agreed with McManus and
awarded McManus Corp 2.1M in damages
for the current loss of revenue and
future potential losses.*

Stephanie wanted to vomit. *$2.1 million in damages?* What
was she going to do? October 2026, that was next year. Was
it over her confrontation in the office? What happened to
Shelby? Stephanie had to sit down.

"I only knew about it because it was a story about another writer. It made me sick because if one company could attack a writer over what one could write, who's to say we are not all at risk?"

"You're telling me."

"So, what happened, Stephanie?"

Stephanie explained the confrontation in the office and how she took a stand for herself, Shelby, and the business. She felt she needed to because she'd had no difficulty with the client before and they were a profitable company—up until that point. She didn't think a change was warranted and thought she was doing a good thing. She didn't realize that McManus would go that far.

"Wow," Aaron said. "I have always wondered about the other side of that story. Amazing that I can get to talk to the one who was there. That's a bum deal, Stephanie."

"The thing is, I don't feel I did anything wrong. I'm half thinking of fighting for it."

"Even knowing that this lawsuit is waiting for you?"

"I don't know, Aaron. They're my biggest client."

"But there are other fish in the sea. Other clients who will not treat you the way this one would."

Stephanie chewed on Aaron's words. "My whole business is built around this client. They are my longest termed and the largest paying."

"But are they worth the headache knowing how they would treat you if things were to go sideways the way they apparently did?" Aaron pointed at the screen. "Who's to say it wouldn't happen another way if it wasn't this incident? Who knows what you wrote or did? This happens."

"I know they wanted to dissolve our relationship over

rates. That's what our meeting was over—rates," Stephanie said.

"Rates are your decision. But in my experience; you give them an inch—they take a mile. You lower it once, who's to say they won't come back the next year looking to cut expenses again. But, consider this. You can agree to *this* rate cut and, in the meantime, build your client base to replace them. That can help you, so you are not relying solely on them as your foundation."

"That makes sense," Stephanie said.

"Then if they ask for another revision, you have no issue because you already have other streams of income," Aaron reassured.

Stephanie nodded, feeling strengthened. "Thank you, Aaron. That makes a lot of sense. I have been so focused on keeping them that I never considered other options. It will hurt a bit, and I will need to make some company adjustments on my end, but all it would take is finding a few new clients."

"There you go," Aaron said. "Get back on the horse."

"I can't lose my business."

"Make plans, and you won't. Do what you need to do, and you will succeed."

Stephanie chuckled. "Sounds like someone needs to take his own advice," she looked around the half-darkened Davies Deli. "If this is what you are called to do, you need to continue it, whether Mom and Pop are here or not. *Your* plans will succeed. From what you have told me so far, you got this. You just need to get your team together and pick up where he left off. You said you have everything you need. You just have to do it."

Aaron looked to the ground, then around, "You're right.

I have just known Pop for so long and so short; that it will be difficult to go on without him. I see his face everywhere. I hear his voice calling me 'my boy.' My dad has been gone since I was little. To me, Pop was my father. I have sat in that chair for the last ten years, hearing him laugh and sing through the window there, watching his hat dance." Aaron again fought off tears. "I just miss him."

"I know it's hard," Stephanie agreed with a sigh. "I didn't know you lost your parents early on. I did too. I grew up depending on nothing but myself. One of my Little Reminders was a typewriter spool. It reminded me of my early successes. That I can succeed when all the odds are against me. I am confident that you also received those reminders, Carter or not."

"Carter gave you a Little Reminder about your past?"

Stephanie laughed. "He took me to my high school newspaper job. There was a typing spool in my desk drawer that had no purpose for being there. It was from a typewriter my aunt, whom I lived with after my parents passed, gave me to use."

"Good grief. So, you are on some kind of Charles Dickens type of flight then?" Aaron said.

Stephanie laughed. "Yes, I guess I am. Eesh. You're not a ghost, are you?"

"No, Carter would be the ghost. And I can assure you he is far from a ghost."

"I can attest to that. He pinched me," Stephanie cringed, rubbing her arm.

"Carter pinched you?" Aaron laughed.

"Well, I accused him of all of this being a dream. He assured me that it wasn't."

"That would do it, I suppose," Aaron said, shaking his with laughter.

"So what's next? I don't know where to go from here. I feel something needs to happen. Each time I visit somewhere, I find something and suddenly vanish back to Carter in the hotel where we are holding hands."

"You're holding hands?

"Yeah. Like some weird séance."

"Heh, well, if that is how God wants to work, who am I to say differently? He allowed Peter to see a dropped blanket of food in a trance, vanished Phillip from the Ethiopian, raptured Enoch and Elijah, and gave John the entire book of Revelation in a vision. God can work however He chooses."

"I don't know about that. But we began to pray, and I was in the past. Then I was back with him for a while and walking along the beach. Then we prayed again, and now I am here with you. That is all I know. I don't know what to expect. But with each experience, I found something. You called them Little Reminders. I just haven't found anything here yet."

"Hmmm. I don't know." Aaron shrugged. "It could be the newspaper article about what happened to you. Or… I hate to be so bold, but knowing Carter and having a history with him, maybe *I* could be the Little Reminder? I've been one before, with a past client of Carter's. He tends to do that." Aaron looked to the ceiling, "I don't know why."

The room started to fade around Stephanie, and Aaron's head tilted. "Cool," Aaron said.

"Relax," Stephanie could hear a distant Carter say. You are almost back. "Remain calm, and everything will be fine."

Aaron faded into the tunnel of darkness, and she wondered if she just evaporated in front of him like a *Star Trek* character beaming to her ship. Then she rematerialized, and she was sitting across from Carter. Her post-trip headache had returned, and the lights' brightness hit her hard. Her hand went to her face to shield her eyes.

"There is water on the table for you," Carter said.

"Thank you," Stephanie said. "Am I home now?"

"Just about," Carter said. "I need you to see something first. Then we can decide what we are going to do."

Chapter
Twenty

Sunday, November 23, 2025

"**W**hat are we doing here, Carter?" Stephanie asked. She couldn't tell where they were, but it was dark and warm, and it smelled of liquor.

"Just sit back and wait. All will be revealed in a moment. Just…"

"…be patient," they both said in unison.

Stephanie nodded, waving her hand in front of her.

"See, now you understand," Carter said.

"What can I get the two of you?" the waitress asked, eyeing the two of them as an odd match.

"Iced water," Carter said.

"The same," Stephanie answered.

"Riiiiiight," the barmaid said, walking away with a headshake.

"We stick out like a sore thumb, Carter. Would you please tell me why we are here?"

"Any moment now."

"This better be worth it," Stephanie said.

"I just need to warn you, though—" Carter began.

"Oh man," Stephanie said. "Is this going to be like the restaurant?"

"In a way."

"So, we are waiting for that pompous jerk to walk in here?"

"You could say that," Carter said.

"Let's get out of here," Stephanie said, attempting to stand, but Carter took her arm and gently pulled her back down.

"Stephanie. Be patient. This will be worth it, I promise. But I need you to do something for me."

"What is that," Stephanie said.

"No matter what happens. Don't react. Just sit here, allow it to happen, and then you and I will leave here the same way we came in. Understand?"

Stephanie stared at Carter. His grey eyes were serious. More serious than she had ever seen. He needed her to obey his request. *This must be important.* "I understand."

"Good," Carter said, his voice lighter. He sipped his water the waitress had delivered and dropped a sizable tip on the table. "I wonder if they have any of those pretzels around?"

A few moments later, raucous noise sounded toward the door. A familiar figure appeared with a tall blonde on his arm. He seemed inebriated from his stammering and stumbling around the room. However, folks in the room seemed to know who he was, greeting him by name. It was no surprise. Everyone here knew who Kenneth Alistair was.

The bartender called to him, she couldn't hear their exchange from where she was, but he apparently wasn't taking a *Mr. Alistair* from her.

There was another familiar figure sitting at the bar

wearing a coat that resembled one she had seen a hundred times before. No, it couldn't be. It wasn't an unusual coat. There could be a thousand coats just like that one out there. It was the neon lights playing tricks with her eyes. But the figure's style and posture made him appear even more familiar.

Then Kenneth corrected the bartender

That figure spun around, and Stephanie stared at the face of her husband.

Sunday, November 23, 2025

"So, what are you lookin' at, bub?" Kenneth challenged Jason.

Jason was staring at the woman on Kenneth's arm, both startled and relieved to see that it wasn't Stephanie.

"Where's Stephanie?"

"Who?" Kenneth's slurred answer indicated he was obviously drunk.

"My wife? Your boss? The woman you came down here with?" Jason spoke his assumption, but now that he didn't see Stephanie, his assumption sounded hollow in his own ears.

"Stephanie? Buddy, you can have her. She dropped me like yesterday's taco. Led me on with promises of fun and games, but the moment the action was set to take place, *poof!* She was nowhere to be found."

Maybe she had second thoughts, Jason mused. *Maybe I do still mean something to her.*

"But you *did* come down here together?"

"Difference does it make?" he slurred. "She's gone. I don't know where, and I don't care. I have this beauty beside me, and the night is just getting started. So if you will excuse us, we would like to get a drink."

Jason stepped aside and let Kenneth pass. He was about to leave when he heard Kenneth call him out.

"Dos Equis? What kinda wuss drinks Dos Equis?" Kenneth turned with Jason's half-empty bottle in his hand. "No wonder your old lady stepped out on you and went looking for a real man. I run into it all the time." He took a few more steps toward Jason, pointing at him with the beer bottle. "Guys like you are not doing business at home, so they need Kenneth to finish the job and close the deal. Well, it is her loss for skipping out anyhow. Probably a sorry lay, anyhow. Probably why you stayed away too."

Jason saw red, and with all the energy he had built-up, he released his frustration into Kenneth's obnoxious mouth. Kenneth staggered back, fell to the floor, and didn't get back up. His blonde girlfriend looked down at the pile of what was left of her date; she reached for his wallet, found his gold card, and handed it to the bartender, "Drinks on him!" she said.

Jason couldn't believe what he had just done. He had never hit a man before. He had thought about it but never acted on the impulse. He had to admit, if only to himself, it felt good! Not only did he deck the guy who was sneaking around with his wife, but he defended his wife's honor. He had thought of her above himself. It was something he hadn't done in a long time. He just wished she was there to see it.

Sunday, November 23, 2025

"You have got to be kidding me," Stephanie nearly yelled.

"Now you promised, Stephanie," Carter said. "You cannot leave this booth."

"But I have to go to him. Did you see what he did?"

"That I did. And you will get to see him. Just not now. He's still sorting things out. Let him."

Then it hit her. She understood it all.

"He knows everything. That's why he's here."

"Yes."

"How did he find out?"

"Because he loves you. He put everything together as a caring husband would. Like a husband who pays attention to his wife would. Remember, you said that you didn't think he paid any attention to you anymore? Well, this is proof that he does. Or if he didn't before, he has learned to again."

"And it proves Kenneth didn't care for me at all. I was lucky I slept through it, or you pulled me away from it," Stephanie admitted.

"Everyone makes decisions. Both good and bad. Even when we find ourselves in the middle of a bad choice, there are always points when we can choose to turn around and run away from those situations. We only need to recognize when those flags are raised and choose to run when we see them."

"I need to find him, Carter. I need to tell him I still love him and that all this was a mistake. I know that now."

"Give it a moment. Let what just happened here process for him. He's coming to grips with your relationship too, Stephanie. Drink some water; you're going to need it." Carter said.

Stephanie did as she was told. The water was tepid, and she wasn't sure if the glass wasn't thoroughly washed or if the glass had been filled with alcohol so much that it had a permanent stain of flavor, but she could taste the previous drink it held.

She momentarily wondered if Carter was getting ready to slip her back into another dimension, but nothing happened. After a few more minutes of music-filled silence, Carter spoke.

"Do you remember everything?"

"It seems like a psychedelic trip, but yes, I do."

"Good. Carry it with you, Stephanie. Everything you learned matters. Every Little Reminder you carry matters. Jason matters. Your kids matter. Your job, whether you keep a client or lose them all, it all results from the choices you make. You must rely on God to help you make those choices. You can do it with Him or without Him, but I can assure you with Him will be much easier. And with your husband." Carter nodded to the door. "The two of you will make an awesome team. You've done it before. You just got lost in the confusion of life. Find your way back, together."

Stephanie knew Carter was right. She had discovered that through every experience and every Little Reminder she picked up along the way. The ribbon and shell reminded her of the dreams she once held, and her husband was there every step, her faithful cheerleader. He never had an ulterior motive for his support but to see her succeed. And she wouldn't be where she was if it weren't for his support. She loved him for that.

"I need to go, Carter," Stephanie said.

"Of course you do," Carter said. "Go. Go find your husband."

Stephanie beamed, stood up, and started for the door, then stopped and turned back to Carter. "Where are you headed now?"

Carter shrugged. "Around. That gelato place opens in the morning. Maybe I will get some sleep and grab some before I head out."

"Will I see you again?"

"If all goes well, I hope not," Carter smiled.

Stephanie laughed, "That sounds optimistically rude."

"You get that in my line of business." Carter laughed. "You better go. He is getting further away."

"Where is he?"

"You know exactly where he is. Now go."

Stephanie smiled. "I'm sure I do," she said and left the bar.

The barmaid returned. "Your date left."

Carter laughed. "She wasn't my date."

"I'm off in a couple of hours; you want one?"

"I'm not the dating type, my dear. But you flatter me, you really do. God bless you."

Sunday, November 23, 2025

Stephanie walked through the 2025 lobby—her time. She wasn't entirely sure what Carter meant by she would know. She doubted that Jason would go up to the room. He didn't know which one she was in. She looked at the restaurant—it was closed. The lobby was also empty. She didn't think he would go to his truck and sit there. The boardwalk would be closed, and she remembered the rudimentary gating around it.

The beach.

Stephanie darted out of the hotel's front entrance and down the walkway to the sand. The air was warmer than she expected, even though a sea breeze was blowing in. She looked toward the water, but the darkness didn't reveal anything or anybody. She had to choose which route she would go if she were him. She closed her eyes and thought about him building a house. He usually worked to his right. Stephanie shrugged and headed toward the water, then in the direction she hoped he would be.

The waves crashed along the shoreline as Stephanie's feet splashed through the foam and receding current. In the distance, she could see a figure a few hundred yards away; tiny, but it was definitely a person. Stephanie didn't want to yell. What if it wasn't him? She would frighten the person, but then again, someone running full steam at you probably wasn't comforting either.

"Jason," Stephanie shouted.

The figure did not divert its attention; it just kept walking.

Stephanie kept moving forward, like a running back determined to reach the goal line.

"Jason," she called again.

This time the figure stopped and turned around.

"Jason. It's me."

"Stephanie?" Jason shouted back.

Stephanie could make out the coat. It was most certainly her husband. The closer she got to him, the more she lost herself. They fell into each other, and the warmth of his embrace overwhelmed her. She had forgotten how welcoming his arms were and how much she longed for his touch. "I found you," she said.

"We found each other."

Neither released the embrace, savoring the moment. Stephanie wasn't sure if he was feeling what she felt—realizing the completion of a journey of loss and redemption. She hated herself for what she had put them through but was grateful for the experience. Now she knew where she belonged and would never let go of what she had. Never.

"I love you, Jason."

"I love you too, Steph." Jason released their embrace. He brushed her hair behind her ear. "You okay?"

"I am now. And I'm sorry."

"For what?"

"For everything. For lying to you. For making mistakes. For letting life get in the way. For being here, for putting you through all of this. You deserve better."

"And I owe you the same apology, Stephanie. I put you in the same position. I've neglected you. I made you feel unloved. That will never happen again. You have my word on it."

Jason leaned into her lips and kissed her like that first day on the beach when he gave her the shell.

She received him like the day she realized he would be the man she would spend the rest of her life with. First kisses had a way of being electrifying and revealing. They could tell you a lot about someone; they could remind you a lot about someone. This Little Reminder connected them to their past and introduced them to their future.

They parted, and Stephanie pulled the shell out of her pocket and handed it to Jason.

"Is this what I think it is?"

"I believe it is," Stephanie said.

"But how? Ours was broken. Josh…"

"I don't ask questions. I just found it, and it was explained to me that it was a favor and a blessing from the Lord," Stephanie said, hoping that would appease him.

Jason's eyes lit up.

"What?"

He took her hand and nearly pulled her arm out of its socket, "Come on. I have something for you too."

"Jason," Stephanie shrieked, nearly falling over.

"Just come on, it's important."

Stephanie followed him, hand in hand, stopping him once they reached the boardwalk to catch her breath.

"You aren't the only one who discovered mysterious gifts. I've been busy myself. Just wait until you see the gift I have for you. You think the menu was crazy? Come on."

He reached for her hand.

"Nuh-uh," Stephanie said with a laugh. "I'll follow. My arm is still sore from the first leg of this journey."

Jason laughed. "Just keep up, dear."

Jason ran back to his pickup, and Stephanie did her best to remain in step with him. He opened the driver's side door and reached inside.

"Are you ready for this?"

"Will you just show me already?"

Jason handed her the Neapolitan square.

"You have got to be kidding me?"

"Nope."

"Where did you find this?"

"At one of those swap meets Dad likes to go to. Mom encouraged me to meet up with him yesterday, and when I found him, we walked the place. Then, in the middle of a stack of crime novels, this stuck out among them. Amazing, right?"

"I wonder how it got there?"

"I have no clue," Jason said.

"It was strange too. Before I found it, I was looking for my dad but couldn't find him. Then I met this codger, and we start a conversation, and he talks about missed opportunities in life. Then my dad shows up, we walk around, and I find your Bible."

"Wait, what?"

"My dad and I were at a swap meet when I found it."

"No, before that. The old codger," Stephanie said.

Jason sighed.

"Talk, mister."

"He started to talk about being sent by God to tell me about you being in trouble. I was scared, so I packed up and started down here. During my drive, I realized how much I've neglected you and how I need to change and be the man I should be for you."

"Did this man have a name?" Stephanie asked.

"He said his name was Carter Jennings. He was tall, snow-white hair. With…"

"…a brown tweed hat and matching coat," Stephanie finished. "Yes. That's the man who—" Stephanie wasn't sure how much more to share.

"Returned the menu," Jason answered for her.

"Yes. That's him."

"He also said that you were okay, and I shouldn't worry about you. But others, like Vanessa, seemed to have something to worry about. But from everything I've seen tonight, I think I would trust Carter and you above what anything anyone would say."

Stephanie wiped tears from her eyes. "I *am* okay. I may have come down here with the wrong intentions. But whatever Carter did—whatever God did—showed me that you are more important to me than anyone else and that whatever hardship we may face, we can work through it. I'm sorry for what I've done. Please forgive me."

"And I'm sorry for allowing you to feel neglected enough to feel the need to find another man's arms attractive."

They stood there gazing into each other's eyes, enjoying the salty air and the sound of the distant waves. He kissed her on the forehead and held her.

"So, are we good, babe?" Jason asked as he released her.

"Yeah, we're good," Stephanie said, then smiled. She looked at her car, then his truck, "Race you home?"

Epilogue
One

Monday, November 23, 2025

Stephanie had yet to see Kenneth. It didn't matter. She had already made her decision. South Carolina is an at-will state, and she had all her employees sign a contract up front stating that she could terminate employment at will. It was the nature of the beast in the marketing/advertising game—all it took was one complaint from a client, and they could lose it all. It took Carter and their adventure to remind her of that.

She had gotten back to their home a half hour before Jason did. His truck may have muscle, but her car had more pep. Before the engine had time to cool down, she was in their study typing up Kenneth's termination paperwork.

They were both tired and restless, but they agreed they needed to be back at church since it was Sunday morning. It had been a long time since they had attended together, but Carter had convinced both of them that they needed to put God first in all things, especially in their relationship. After a quick shower, they were out the door. Their pastor was overjoyed to see them—together and in the same vehicle. He commented on how much lighter they both appeared. They thanked him and took their seats on the pew.

Vanessa had not mentioned Jason's calls to her or anything about Kenneth. None of the team had asked about him; yet. She knew she would eventually have to address it, or gossip would ensue, and a team that gossips gets disconnected, and then you lose control. She did not need that on her watch. She would also have to tell them about losing one of their biggest clients and encourage them that they would get through it.

"I have the proofs for the EverYear Tire piece," Vanessa said as she entered the room with a stack of images. "I talked to Randy, and he approved. We just need to line out the copy." Vanessa stood at the front of her desk with a questioning look.

Stephanie's mind clicked. EverYear was Kenneth's account. It was one of the pieces he submitted before he left for the weekend.

"Close the door, Vanessa," Stephanie said.

Vanessa turned and looked at the door, looked back to her, and then complied.

"Boss, I'm not going to say—"

"Before you continue, Vanessa, I want to thank you for your discretion. It is admirable. But I also want to apologize for placing you in that position. It was unforgivable for me to do that. I am a married woman who was doing things she—"

"Mrs. Marshall," Vanessa attempted to interrupt.

"Please let me finish. I need to say this. I owe it to you."

"Okay."

"First, Kenneth will no longer be working with Marshall Copywriting. I have his release paperwork here. Please make sure it is sent out by certified mail as soon as possible."

Stephanie handed her the sealed envelope.

Vanessa accepted the document.

"Second, I need you to know that nothing happened between us. Yes, we did go to the coast with every intention. But when things got down to it…." Stephanie trailed off. How would she explain Carter? "Things just didn't happen."

"Good for you, ma'am," Vanessa said with a bright smile. "I was praying for you."

"Well, it worked. You have no idea how much it worked." Stephanie smiled. "And I know my husband nagged you all night long. I'm sorry for that as well."

"He by no means pestered me. I will be honest, my husband wasn't too happy about another man calling me after hours, but when I explained the situation, he was less irritated."

"Thank you for helping him. He might not have found me if it weren't for you."

"He wouldn't have known about you meeting Kenneth either. I'm afraid I let that slip, too," Vanessa explained.

"Good. I'm glad. He needed to know. If it weren't for that, he wouldn't have fought as hard as he did."

"That was my husband, Gary. He said I should just tell him."

"How ever the decision was made, I'm grateful. It lit a fire that made him more determined to find me."

"Then I am grateful, too," Vanessa said. "I knew Kenneth was up to no good. I always wanted to warn you. But I didn't think it was my place. After all, you are a grown woman—and you're my boss. But looking back, I wish I had. Maybe you wouldn't have had to go through all that trauma. So, I am sorry."

"Don't be. There are no hard feelings, and we are okay. I mainly wanted you to understand everything because of what you saw, and I wanted you to know that I have gotten my life straight with God *and* with Jason. I was saved."

"You must've had a guardian angel that protected you."

Stephanie laughed. "You don't know the half of it."

Epilogue
Two

Thursday, November 26, 2025

"I cannot believe this," Jason said. "Look at this line?"

"I know, right? How can this many people fit in that double-wide?" Stephanie said.

The place looked different in the daylight. The first time she saw it, it was pitch dark, five years from now. She was worried about how she would introduce herself to Aaron. She already knew he wouldn't know her. But she knew so much about him.

"So, in your, um—dream-like trance—you were here? And you met the owner?"

"Will you keep quiet? People can hear you, Jason," Stephanie said, looking around. The two businessmen behind them were engaged in a conversation about their next meeting at two. One was concerned about making the meeting; the other said he didn't care if they had to reschedule because Pops turkey was worth missing the appointment for.

Stephanie had to laugh under her breath.

The couple in front of them were obviously on the other spectrum. Meetings were definitely *not* on their agenda. Perhaps the warmth of the building was as welcome as the meal.

"So, do you have a plan for what you will write yet?"

"I'm getting there. Seeing all of this gives me a start. Perhaps it will give an entrepreneur an idea of starting one of these on the East Coast. There is need all over the place for hearts like this family has."

"And you say the owner passes away in five years?"

"*Jason*," Stephanie snapped.

"Oh, sorry." Jason lowered his voice. "But the co-owner will take over and will not be sure if he can?"

"Yeah, but from what I am seeing, he needs to. Look at all of this, Jason. If he were to stop, all these people wouldn't get fed. He said that this year they would feed fifteen hundred. The year before I visited him, they fed two thousand. *Two thousand*, Jason. That is more than what you will see today. He can't stop now."

"Or then," Jason said.

"Now you're getting it," Stephanie said.

The line moved steadily; they were now in line with the front windows. Stephanie could see all the patrons sitting and eating at the booths, smiling, chatting, and enjoying their meals.

"Just wait until you see the inside of this place. It will blow your mind," Stephanie said, but she could already see something inside that had Jason's attention. "What is it?

"I don't know. The guy who is taking names. I could swear I've seen him before," Jason said.

"The big guy?" Stephanie said.

"Yeah. He looks familiar."

"You work with a lot of contractors and their workers; maybe on a job site?" Stephanie said.

"In Houston?"

"Oh. Hmm. Well, I'm not sure then," Stephanie looked at the tall Black man taking names at a podium.

"Don't think I've seen him. Maybe he is a journeyman. They get around. You can ask him when we get inside. He could be doing this to help out for the holiday," Stephanie suggested.

Jason nodded, but he wasn't buying it. Stephanie could tell.

The line continued to move, and they talked about the trip over and how they enjoyed the scenery of Mississippi and Louisiana. She mentioned that she should tell Lauren about her adventure and suggest the two areas she ran across and get stories written about them. The line moved them through the doors, and they welcomed the warmth. Then they found themselves next in line. The maître d' was scribbling on his pad and then looked up at them. He scrunched his face looking at Jason.

"I know you," the man said.

"I was thinking the same thing, but I can't place your face," Jason said. "Who are you?"

"My name is Derrick. I work at a bookstore, but I volunteer here for Thanksgiving meal."

"Derrick," Jason said. Then he snapped his fingers. "The Peninsula Church."

"The lost pickup," Derrick said. "Wow, small world. How are you? Guess you found your way."

"That I did," he said, glancing toward his wife.

Derrick looked to Stephanie. "Good afternoon, miss. I'm Derrick."

"I'm sorry," Jason said, with a laugh, "This is my wife, Stephanie."

"Good to meet you, Derrick," Stephanie said.

"Pleasure is mine. So, there will be two of you today?"

"Yes," Jason said.

"Okay. It shouldn't be too long. You can wait wherever you can find a seat here."

Jason led her to one of the benches set up in the lobby. He told her about meeting Derrick in the parking lot before going into the church.

"Derrick was the one who led me inside. I had forgotten about him until I saw his face in the window. He mentioned he was from South Texas. He was with his fiancée, Breonna."

"Wow," Stephanie said. "That is amazing."

"You said the pastor you spoke to told you that you stopped in that parking lot for a reason. That there was a purpose to it."

"Yeah, but I didn't think that purpose was to meet a guy I'd come across here in Texas. That visit was to get answers for you, for us. Meeting him was just an added bonus. The pastor and I exchanged numbers. He's looking to build soon. I'm may assist in that build. God orchestrated that stop in more ways than one. Perhaps God sent Derrick to that church to get him excited about what they are doing there as well. Who knows what the future holds there?"

"Who knows," Stephanie echoed.

A waitress came and led them to a booth near the rear of the restaurant. A couple was sitting in the next booth with a dark-haired female facing away from them; she was talking quite feverishly, and both adults had giant smiles on their faces, the look parents have when they are proud of a child's accomplishment. Stephanie knew that look. It was one she had always hoped to see from a parent. She was overjoyed for the child enjoying the holiday with their parents.

"I'm Jasmine, and I'll be your server," the waitress introduced herself. "Tea, coffee, soft drink?"

"Tea," Jason said.

Stephanie smiled. "I know he may be swamped, but can you see if Aaron can make his special cocoa?"

Jasmine smirked and said, "I will see what I can do."

"*Special* cocoa?" Jason said.

"Oh, don't go reading too much into that. It was something his wife made for him. He made it for me because I was lost in the cold and was he comforting me as I told him our story."

"Gotcha," Jason said.

Jasmine returned with tea for Jason. "Aaron is in the back," she said to Stephanie. "I'm going to find him now."

Stephanie nodded.

As she left, Derrick passed them and greeted the family behind them. Seconds later, the chatty female stepped out of the booth, "Hello, sir. I'm Breonna. We met that night too. I'm Derrick's fiancée."

"That's right. I remember you," Jason said. "When's the big date?"

"Right around the corner. January 23."

"That's great. It must be exciting."

"Yes. We've been dating a year now, figured it was time to tie the knot," Breonna said. "Derrick graduates soon, and we just want to be set."

"Well, double congratulations then," Stephanie said.

Jason shook Derrick's hand. "Yes, sir. Congratulations. What will your degree be in?"

"Psychology and Children's Education," Derrick said. "I plan to be a social worker."

"Ah, you will be involved with community programs like this quite a bit."

"I hope to," Derrick said.

"We will keep you in prayer," Jason said.

"We appreciate that."

"I see the two of you have met," an approaching voice said. Aaron patted Derrick on the shoulder. "Things are really moving along. I think we will break last year's record, Derrick. Thank you so much for helping again this year."

"No problem. It's my pleasure," Derrick said. "I hope to make it a regular thing."

"That would be a blessing."

"We will let you get back to your family," Stephanie said. "It was good to meet you."

"Good to meet you as well," Derrick said.

"Yes. It was," Breonna said, giving them one of her glowing smiles.

Jason, Stephanie, and Aaron exchanged pleasantries. Then Aaron set down a steaming cup of cocoa in front of Stephanie and pulled up a chair.

"There aren't many people who know about this concoction," Aaron said. "And I've lived enough these past few years to know there are no such things as coincidences. So, I know you are not here by chance. Either Derrick told you about my late wife's cocoa, which he just assured me he did not, or another less likely source did."

"Would you believe me if I said that *you* told me about it?" Stephanie said.

Aaron bit the corner of his mouth. "Well, that's a new one.

I don't remember telling anyone about it—other than Derrick. And I only told him about it because he doesn't like coffee."

Stephanie chose to take a chance. Since he knew Carter, perhaps he would be able to believe the unbelievable. "Would you believe you don't remember because you haven't told me about it yet."

"How does that work?"

"You won't tell me about it for another five years," Stephanie said through gritted teeth.

"And tell me. Would a white-haired, tweed-wearing angelic being have anything to do with this," Aaron said.

Stephanie smiled. "Most definitely."

Aaron looked to the ceiling, "Why don't you just tell me you are going to do these things, so I'm prepared?" Then back to Stephanie. "So, time travel? Carter is doing time travel now?"

"He figures it more future glimpses of what could be considered Charles Dickens-type stuff."

"Ghost of Christmas Future." Aaron nodded.

"Hah! That's what I said. But he said he was no ghost."

"Yeah, Carter is anything but a ghost."

"He pinched me to prove it," Stephanie said, leaning into the table and rubbing her arm.

"He pinched you?"

Stephanie laughed. "You are reacting the same way you will react in five years."

"I would assume I wouldn't change who I am?"

"He wanted to prove that I wasn't dreaming when I challenged him."

"But why did he bring you to me and Davies Deli in the future?"

Stephanie still wasn't quite sure how to answer the question, although it was the very reason why she had come. A phone call would not do. She needed to meet Aaron face-to-face to encourage him to continue in the face of Pop's death, without telling him about Pop's death. Most of all, she needed to see the deli for herself. Maybe she could use her influence to send a spark into what was going on here in her part of the world. She wasn't trying to be prideful, but she realized she had a certain level of clout, and she had a responsibility to use it to help those who needed the shoulder to stand on. It was her calling.

It was that sense of call which had gotten lost in over the last few years. She planned to fix that. And it all started with Davies Deli.

"First, I need to begin by telling you that I am a writer like you. I write freelance, but I also own my own business, Marshall Copywriting. I built it up bit-by-bit by writing small articles for pennies. Now I employ four writers, and we have clients up and down the eastern seaboard."

"Is that right?" Aaron said. "Impressive."

"I now know I was one of Carter's Little Reminders causes. He wanted to expose me to what *could be* from what *once was*. I had gotten so lost in who I was as a writer, Aaron, that I forgot why I even started. I then learned that you are a writer, and you still do all of this and manage to keep your head on straight.

"I need that focus in my life. And I found that process through our discussion. No matter what comes my way, I can do what I need to do. Writing is my calling. My husband and children are my calling. And when God is the focal point, everything falls into place. You reminded me of that. I thank Carter for directing me to you to help me remember."

Aaron nodded. "Carter has a way of opening our eyes to what we are blind to. God uses him in amazing ways. I'm glad he helped you find your way home." Aaron was silent a moment, then chuckled. "Anything else you can tell me about the future, Ms. McFly?"

Stephanie chose to keep everything else to herself. Pop's passing, Aaron's questioning the Deli's future, and his working through it. It was his battle, and having that insight now would only complicate his path over the next five years. What she went through was for her alone. It hurt not to be able to tell him. It occurred to her that she hadn't thought about the dancing hat in the kitchen window. She didn't want to look now. If she did, she would burst into tears, and then Aaron would know. And she didn't want him to know that Pop had a five-year expiration date.

"You know what I know. Keep on keeping on, Aaron. This place will continue to succeed far beyond what you are seeing now. That I can tell you. Prepare for that. Just never give up on this place, no matter what." Stephanie winked at him.

"You have my word," Aaron said. He looked around. "Just promise you will write about this place to your east coasters."

"You can count on it," Stephanie said.

Epilogue
Three

The park was clear of heavy traffic, just as the earthbound angel preferred it. Carter Jennings sat on a park bench, enjoying the sun rising over the horizon. The morning was crisp but not too cold, not that the temperature affected him much. Houston never got that cold to begin with.

Why Gabriel chose here to meet was not that complicated. He knew Carter enjoyed it here. If he were human, this would be the place he'd like to settle down and call home. Three of his favorite places on earth were here. The library, the coffee stand in front of the library, and Davies Deli. Carter's tastebuds and stomach fought each other for which wanted attention first.

A hooded figure jogged toward Carter, making him laugh to himself. His friend was getting better at blending in.

"Good morning, Gabriel," Carter said.

"How did you know it was me?"

"You have that… glow about you," Carter jested.

Gabriel looked around him. He had hidden his appearance well. Even his locks of hair were well hidden.

"You're fine, Gabe. It's just a phrase. So, how are you this morning?"

"The better question is, how are *you*?"

"I am well. This last assignment was an interesting one. I'm grateful to have been part of it. I was unaware that our Lord still worked in that fashion."

"He works in all ways that draw people to Him," Gabriel said.

"Understandable," Carter nodded. "I am honored that He trusted me with such an assignment."

"You were the only one He *could* trust with it. No one thinks outside the box the way you do. For that, He is grateful. He does think it is time, though."

"Time? Time for what?"

"Time for you to come home." Gabriel lowered his hoodie and met Carter's eyes.

"I don't understand. Did I do something wrong?"

"Not at all. Your performance has been exemplary. But after one hundred years of guiding souls back to Him, it's time for a break. It's time to come home and see why you continue to remind those who are still here. Remember, you are earth-bound. You are tied to this world with its emotions and the decisions humans make. Don't you ever miss Heaven and being in His presence?"

"Of course, I do. But there is so much work to do here. So many who need people, and angels, like me," Carter said.

"And another earth-bound will take your place. Another who will have a heart like yours to provide those Little Reminders and draw people back to Christ."

Carter looked around the park. Two runners were a distance off, probably trying to reach a new best time. A squirrel scampered up a tree. Horns honked in the distance from the hustle and bustle of city driving.

"I will miss this place."

"When you step into the presence of Christ, all of this won't matter compared to the beauty of the Lord," Gabriel said.

"I know. But still. I have grown attached to helping them all."

"It may not be forever. Remember, we are stepping out of time. It doesn't mean there won't be a point where you will be asked to step back into it."

Carter nodded and grinned. "Too bad they don't make heavenly garments like this," Carter spun around, showing off his coat and cap one final time."

"Let's be grateful they don't, Carter."

Gabriel looked around. Both the runners and the squirrel were long gone. He closed his eyes, and blinding light surrounded him, and his hoodie and sweatpants vanished as his white robe, and woolen blond hair returned. He opened his blue eyes and smiled.

"Much better," Gabriel said. "Those other garments were stuffy."

Carter laughed. "Do I really get to do that now?"

"All you need to do is accept that your mission here is complete, and God will return your heavenly status."

Carter grinned and closed his eyes. He felt a power like no other. He had heard Gabriel tell others that there were no words to describe Heaven and God's power. He was correct. Words like peace, serenity, love, joy, and passion were all small and finite compared to what he was experiencing. He could understand Gabriel's smile when the change from limited to infinite occurred. He felt the weight of human emotion dissolve—rather *evolve*—into something that was no longer a burden but an asset that allowed him to empathize. It was no longer something that could get in the way and cloud his judgment. He understood, he grasped, and he was free.

Carter opened his eyes.

The park was still there, but it looked different. The colors were crisper, the sounds were more true, and the world was more real. He looked down at himself, halfway hoping the coat and cap made the journey, but they hadn't. Like his companion, he wore sparkling white. He felt his face; he still bore his beard and imagined it remained white; it was part of who he was.

"How do you feel, Carter?" Gabriel asked.

"I'm still trying to figure that out," Carter replied. "But I'm beginning to remember. It has been one hundred years, you know."

"Yes. You chose this mission. Once an angel does that, he has to forget what it is like in Heaven, or it will pain him with the separation. It is not for the faint of heart. You made an honorable sacrifice for hundreds of lives, Carter. You gave them so many Little Reminders that changed their lives, brought them back to the Lord, and in turn, brought so many others to Christ. Now it is your turn to rest in Him again."

Gabriel produced a shoebox, just the way Carter handled all his cases. He handed it to Carter. A knowing expression fell across Carter's face. "I remember," Carter said.

"After a hundred years, we tend to forget things, but yes, the shoebox. You chose, rather demanded, to use a shoebox to deliver all of your Little Reminders because—"

Carter finished, "—because of Timothy. He was the teenager we helped. He secretly kept little knickknacks in a shoebox. He called them his little reminders of friends and family."

"Yes," Gabriel said. "After leading him back to God, you were impressed with him and his idea. You pushed the shoebox idea on me and started to call all our deliveries *little reminders.*"

"I can't believe I'd forgotten that," Carter said.

"That's what one hundred years in a human body will do to you, Carter. It's not your fault."

Carter nodded. "Thank you for showing this to me, Gabriel."

"Now it is someone else's turn to begin their journey of helping people find their way back to God, and it's your turn to enjoy your reward."

"Can you do something for me?"

"Sure," Gabriel said.

Carter extended the box to him. "I know a rookie will want to tackle things with fresh new tactics, but if you find an old soul who likes their cases more traditional, let them know this method has been successful."

"I will do that, my friend."

Carter looked around the park one more time, then he turned his face to the sky and smiled. "I guess it's time to go."

"It is. You ready?"

The two angels stood in the center of a park in the middle of Houston, Texas. The world around them would continue. But hearts had been changed, and lives had been set on a straighter course. And whether it be for the patrons of Davies Deli, the readers of the *Houston Gazette*, Marshall Copywriting, LLC, or a book Derrick Anders had reshelved, Carter Jennings had been part of the change that occurred in those lives.

Changes—for the better.

Acknowledgments

It's been an amazing ride, friends. Here we are at the closure of our character stories. I guess if I could pick any particular one of them, excluding Carter, as my favorite, it would be Aaron. He has been the constant of the series. Of course, he had to be a writer, as a way of writing myself into the book. He also had a love for the culinary with the Deli. Who was yours?

I loved writing this series, and penning the end was heart-tugging. I won't say 'breaking' because I can relieve any moment by just cracking a spine. I know you will agree, it's through the power of the written word that every moment is there to be relived.

I want to take a final moment to thank everyone involved in writing this series. I'm not sure why, but I have a heart-pull for Houston. I drove through the city many times as a trucker on my way to Lake Charles, Louisiana, and back to Corpus. I never thought twice about having this series set elsewhere. Even this novel makes a return there. It just had to; Aaron is there. So, thank you Houston. And I'm not even an Astros fan; sorry Altuve.

Next, I want to thank my clients who have given me the chance to write for them. Maurice Draine, you have meant more to my writing career than you know. Without taking a chance on me, I would not be the writer or editor I am today. And to others who have given me a shot to perfect my abilities and the experiences to become a well-rounded writer, thank you.

Then there is Mike Parker here at WordCrafts Press, who gave me the ultimate opportunity to become a published author with a dystopian novel about a man who needed to reconnect with the world around him and paid the penalty for doing so. Then came this series. A love story. Wow. What a journey *Little Reminders* became. Thank you, Mike, and thank you, reader, for allowing it to be such a great success. And now we wrap up the final book in this trilogy.

It would not be an acknowledgment page unless I thank my still the one, Carolyn. She has been my inspiration to keep writing. While amazing enough, she is more partial to my *Transference* series than this one, however, she is the drive to complete every work I endeavor to write. She is my cheerleader and my biggest fan.

Thank you, my Lord and Savior Jesus Christ, for entrusting me with this gift. I could not pen a word or inspire a single person if your Spirit did not influence my life. Thank you for trusting me to spread your Word through prose.

Finally, thank you, reader, for joining me on Carter's journey. I hope you had fun, were inspired, and perhaps cried a bit. I know I did writing this final episode. God bless you. I look forward to hearing your thoughts and reviews.

About the Author

Jeff S. Bray lives in a small town in South Central Texas with his wife Carolyn and two of their five children. They are members of the local First Baptist Church, serving in several capacities, including teaching Sunday School, working with Men's Ministry, and managing the church's online presence.

Jeff's passion for writing began in elementary school with a short story about a lost kitten. His circuitous literary career started with his personal blog, *Moments for the Heart*, which led to small paid assignments before expanding into magazine articles in national publications.

Little Reminders of Who I Was, is the sequel to the supernatural romance, *Little Reminders of Who I Am*. Jeff is also the author of the contemporary thrillers *The Transference* and *The Five Barred Gate*, and the whimsical children's picture book series, *Elissa the Curious Snail*, which helps parents introduce basic faith concepts like prayer, even in the face of adversity, into their teachings in a fun and entertaining way.

Connect with Jeff online at:

jeffsbrayauthor.com

also available from
WordCrafts Press

The Carpenter and His Bride
by Paula K. Parker

Oh, to Grace!
by Abby Rosser

Paint Me Fearless
by Hallie Lee

In Search of the Beloved
by Marian Rizzo

27 Words
by KL Palmer

www.WordCrafts.net